CHAPTER ONE

Hey Matt (aka Einstein wannabe),

How's it going, Dr. Bloomenstein? I can't believe Mom let you set up a mini-science lab in the basement. That's a scary thought. With all those test tubes you've got, you could be creating radioactive cockroaches down there or something. Just be sure to let them loose in Adam's room, not mine, k?

I can't believe there're only two weeks left here at camp. The summer's gone by way too fast. It's such a downer to think about leaving. But I'm still planning on getting in as much fun as possible while I'm here. No, Big Bro, before you start with one of your lectures, this doesn't mean pranks. Since I got in trouble with Dr. Steve last summer for all my pranking (the animal-shack fiasco in particular), I'm breaking new records for good behaviour (even without Stephanie around to play the "Third Parent"... ha-ha). I only raided Adam's cabin once so far — talk about exhibiting amazing self-control. Besides, I've got way more important things to worry about right now.

Colour War starts next week, and I've been putting in some serious preparation time on the soccer field and basketball court. Remember how I was voted MVP for the Blue team last year? It'll be tough to top that, but I'm gonna try! Alex and I have been scrimmaging on the soccer field in all of our free time. She's even better than last year, Matt! I really hope we're on the same colour team again this year. If we are, we might be able to bring home a Lakeview Champion title. Even though we're in different cabins (which was a major bummer at the beginning of the summer) we're still awesome friends like always. And we're ready to kick some big-time Colour War butt!

Anyway, enjoy your — ugh — science. Just don't blow anything up unless it's Mom's spinach casserole. That I can live without. I better sign off. Natalie and Alyssa are threatening to toss my candy stash in the lake if we don't go to dinner RIGHT NOW. Yeesh. They must really be starving if they're this excited about the mess-hall food. I'm just hoping it's not a mystery meat loaf day. I miss you, and I'll see you soon.

Love,

Jenna

Jenna Bloom looked hungrily at the platters of French fries that the CITs, or counsellors-in-training, were marching through the mess hall.

"Are you seriously going to eat those?" her friend Alex asked.

"Yup." Jenna grinned. "They're the only things that look edible." She and Alex had to eat at separate tables with their different bunks, but they always had a few minutes to chat beforehand. She saw Alex sizing up a tray of mac and cheese. "Don't tell me that you're going to *eat* that? It looks a little curdly, if you ask me."

"It doesn't look that bad," Alex said. "But then again, I have to think positive about it, since I'm sick of French fries and this is the only other thing I can eat. Besides the mushy broccoli."

"Sorry about that," Jenna said. "But you're probably way healthier than any of the rest of us, especially me." She knew from their last summer together that Alex had juvenile diabetes and had to be really careful about what she ate. Pasta and vegetables were good for her, but some other kinds of food, especially ones full of sugar, were dangerous for her to eat. But now that all the girls knew about Alex's condition, they were careful to be understanding of it. Jenna grinned and elbowed her playfully. "And if it makes you feel better, I asked my mom to send some honey cookies in the last box of goodies she mailed me. Just for you. The package came this morning, and it's sitting under my bunk...right now. I figured we'd both need some extra energy to perfect our soccer skills for Colour War," Jenna said. "Hey, what did you request for your final electives?"

"I asked for sports and photography," Alex said as they headed towards their tables.

"Photography?" Jenna asked. "I didn't know you were into taking pictures."

Alex blushed. "Well, I – I've been wanting to learn the right way to use my camera for a while now, and... and..." She stammered, and the words died away.

"And you wanted to be in an elective with Adam?" Jenna teased, watching Alex's cheeks flush bubblegum pink. She rolled her eyes. Adam, Jenna's brother, was the camp's best photographer. Last summer, Alex had had a tiny crush on Adam, and every once in a while Jenna still caught Alex looking at Adam with a shy smile on her face. But there was no way Alex could possibly *really* like Adam again, was there?

Alex giggled. "I don't know, I might not even get to be in photography. What electives did you ask for?"

"I asked for sports, too, of course," Jenna said. "If we both get sports, we can practise soccer and basketball every day. Man, if we're on the same colour team, we'll be unstoppable!"

"Lakeview legends, reigning victorious," Alex said. "I can't wait."

"We'll go down in history, that's for sure," Jenna said, slapping her a high five before they split up to sit down at their separate bunk tables. She and Alex had been coming to Camp Lakeview for the past five years, and it seemed like they'd been friends for ever. They'd always been in the same bunk together, until this summer. This summer, all of the girls from last year's bunk 3C had been divided into separate bunks. Jenna was in 4A, and Alex was in 4C. But that hadn't stopped the two of them from staying close friends. Sports were what Jenna and Alex did best, and Jenna couldn't wait to spend as much of her free time with Alex on the soccer field as possible.

Jenna plopped down at 4A's table next to Natalie and Tori, who were in the middle of a debate about Tad Maxwell's latest hairstyle for his new movie, *Spy in the Sahara*. Tad was a huge movie star, but he was also Natalie's dad. He'd shown up at camp once last summer and had practically caused a fainting frenzy of mass proportion among the girls. But for the most part, Nat liked to keep a low profile about him. Except, apparently, today.

"I can't believe he got hair extensions for this movie," Nat said, shaking her head as she looked at Tad's photo in the issue of *Star Scoop* that Tori had brought with her to lunch. "His hair's longer than mine now! And he's middle-aged *and* a parent. That's just not right."

"Maybe the directors wanted him to look younger," Alyssa offered, leaning over the table to inspect the photo. "It's gotta be tough to be over forty and competing with guys like Orlando Bloom for roles. Hollywood isn't very forgiving of wrinkles."

"Well, I think he looks cute," Tori said. "He has to look rugged if he's roughing it on a camel in the desert for this movie."

Nat groaned, her head in her hands. "If anyone else calls my dad 'cute' again, I'm in serious danger of losing my lunch."

"If it makes you feel better, I don't think he's cute," Jenna jumped in. "And I think he looks better with a buzz cut."

"Thank you!" Nat said, snapping the magazine shut.

"No problem." Jenna smiled as she dipped a couple of her French fries in ketchup.

She was just about to pop them into her mouth when Alyssa's eyes widened in horror. "Jenna, stop!"

Jenna froze. "What?" she asked, glancing down at her food. But then she saw it. The charred clump of...

what? A bug? A piece of yesterday's mystery meat loaf? Jenna couldn't tell for sure. But whatever it was, it was stuck to the side of one of the fries looking *very* unappetizing. "Eeeuw!" she cried, flinging the fry back onto her plate in disgust. "How gross is that?" She dumped her fries in the trash and dug into her chicken fingers instead, but only after carefully inspecting them to make sure they were free of UFOs (Unidentified Food Objects) first. "Okay, guys. Word to the wise. Avoid the French fries at all costs."

Just then, Tori gave a low whistle.

"Hottie," she whispered excitedly, "twelve o'clock. Headed this way."

Jenna looked up to see Adam walking towards their table. "Gross, Tori," she said. "My brother is *so* not hot. That's a totally disturbing picture."

"Not Adam," Nat said. "I think Tori means the guy *with* Adam. Who is *he*?"

The stranger walking with Adam hadn't even registered on Jenna's radar before, but now she took a second look as they came closer. Even Jenna had to admit that the blond-haired, blue-eyed guy looked more like a boarding-school preppy than a camper. From the sleek sunglasses perched on his head to his boating shoes and polo shirt, he was primped, polished and could've been straight out of one of those *Star Scoop* photos.

"No way," Tori whispered. "Those *cannot* be Hugo Boss sunglasses he's wearing."

"Hugo who?" Jenna asked.

"It's a store so expensive that my dad refuses to shop there," Nat said. "He thinks it's way overpriced."

"And for your dad the super spy," Alyssa added, "that's saying a lot."

Adam stopped at their table and ruffled Jenna's brown hair before she could stop him. She gave him a shove in return.

"Hey, guys, Dr. Steve asked me to introduce his nephew to everyone here today," Adam explained, nodding to the guy at his side. "This is Blake Wetherly. He's from East Hampton in New York. He's visiting for the last two weeks of camp, and he's bunking with us in 4E."

"Hello, ladies," Blake said after Adam had introduced all the girls. He flashed a brilliant grin worthy of a young Brad Pitt. "Nice to meet you all."

"You too," Nat, Tori, Chelsea and Karen all echoed at once.

Jenna nearly choked on a chicken finger as she looked around the table to see nearly everyone's eyelashes batting in unison at Blake. What was wrong with the world these days, when her friends went off the deep end for a guy wearing a pair of overpriced sunglasses? She sighed.

"I'm going to show Blake the ropes today," Adam explained, "and hopefully he'll get the hang of camp in enough time to get totally prepped for Colour War next week, too."

"Colour War? But, but," Jenna stuttered. "Dr. Steve never lets anyone participate in Colour War unless they've been a camper all summer long." She looked at Blake. "Why didn't you come to camp with everyone else at the beginning of the summer?"

"I was abroad for the last month," Blake said nonchalantly, as if travelling internationally was something he did all the time. Which, Jenna suddenly realized, he probably did. "My parents have a summer house in Lake Como, Italy. We go there every year."

"How amazing! Last summer my parents took me to Paris," Tori chirped, tossing her glossy hair over her shoulder and smiling. "But I've never been to Lake Como. I'd love to hear all about it."

"Sure thing," Blake said. "But I'm starving. My dad's jet landed late. We flew here straight from Rome, and I haven't eaten since this morning. And then the limo got lost on the way here."

"Poor baby," Jenna muttered under her breath.

"This place is really out in the sticks," Blake continued. "My uncle's such a hick. You might be a redneck if you live in a place where the mosquitoes outnumber the people." He laughed as if he'd just told the funniest joke in the world, and Tori, Nat and Karen laughed right along with him.

"Dr. Steve's great," Jenna said with a touch of defensiveness. The way Blake had said the word *hick* made it sound like a fate worse than death, and his attitude suddenly irked Jenna, who loved coming here every year, mosquitoes and all.

"And the bugs aren't too bad," Nat piped up. "I got eaten alive the first week I was here last year, but insect repellent works miracles."

"And reeks, too." Blake crinkled his nose up in distaste. "So, is any of the grub decent around here, or should I break out the Pepto-Bismol?"

Jenna resisted the urge to tell Blake to go jump in the lake and gave him a big grin instead. "Give the French fries a try. They're super-yummy."

"Thanks," Blake said, flashing his gleaming smile again. "I'll catch you guys later at the campfire."

"What a snob!" Jenna exclaimed after Blake walked away with Adam. "If his nose were stuck up any higher in the air, he'd have altitude sickness."

Alyssa laughed. "He did seem a little full of himself."

"Maybe he just feels awkward because he doesn't

know anyone here," Karen offered. "It's gotta be tough to come into camp right at the end of the summer like this."

"Not that tough," Jenna countered. "In fact, I'm guessing Blake hasn't had too many tough times in his life. His dad has a private jet, and a limo to boot? Come on."

"And he lives in the Hamptons," Tori said, whispering the word as if it were too special to say out loud. "My parents have been there before to visit some friends. My mom told me they stayed in a house with twelve bathrooms! Can you imagine?"

"I can. I'd never have to fight Stephanie for the bathroom mirror again," Jenna said dreamily, thinking of her big sister Stephanie's hour-long primping sessions.

"I didn't know you ever looked in the mirror, Jen," Chelsea quipped. "Not with that hair."

Jenna chose to ignore that remark. Chelsea was always saying something snippy, and everyone in the two bunks had learned to take her harsh words with a grain of salt.

"Doesn't Donald Trump have a mansion in the Hamptons?" Karen asked, trying to move past Chelsea's comment.

"Donald Trump has mansions everywhere," Nat

replied, and snuck another look at Blake. "He is cute. But not as cute as Simon, of course."

Nat and Simon were one of the camp's couples, and they'd liked each other since last summer. But Nat was still carrying on the eternal debate of whether or not to actually kiss Simon on the lips. Jenna couldn't imagine getting anywhere near a guy's lips. No way.

Nat lifted the collar of her T-shirt up to her nose. "Does bug spray really smell that bad?"

"*Nat.*" Jenna groaned. "You do *not* smell. And if Blake wants to be all stuck-up about wearing insect repellent, let him be. He'll be covered in bites by tomorrow morning." She giggled at the thought. "And if you guys had brothers as annoying as Adam, you wouldn't think *any* guy was cute."

Jenna sighed. Guys were okay...some of the time, but she wasn't entirely sure she wanted to get bitten by the *lurve* bug any time soon. She'd had a *tiny* crush on her brother's friend David earlier in the summer, but when it turned out he liked Sarah, she'd gotten over it pretty quickly. But Nat, Alex and Tori were a different story – they and over half of Jenna's other friends were involved in major crushes.

Thankfully, just when Jenna was getting tired of the boy talk, Andie and Mia, the bunk's counsellor and CIT, stood up from the table. "Singdown time!" Andie announced with a grin, and suddenly everyone forgot about boys, at least for the moment.

Jenna wiped another sticky string of marshmallow off her chin and popped it into her mouth. Flopping back in the grass, she basked in the warmth of the campfire's glow.

"Mmmm." She gave her friends a goopy smile. "There's nothing better than s'mores."

"Really?" Nat said, taking a big bite out of her s'more sandwich and giggling as some chocolate dribbled down her chin. "I thought you loved brownies more."

"Brownies!" Jenna said longingly. "I love them, too. I bet I could make super s'mores with brownies instead of graham crackers."

"Jenna, is there anything you think about besides food?" Chelsea smirked.

"Right this second, no." Jenna laughed. She scooted over to where Karen and Alyssa sat singing a funny version of "The Bear Went over the Mountain" that they'd turned into "The Camper Got Lost on the Mountain". She threw one arm around each girl and joined in, singing the words at the top of her lungs. Soon, the three girls were hiccuping with laughter in

17

between verses. They'd finished the singdown a while ago, but everyone in the division was still in singing mode, making up silly lyrics to songs and belting them out as the fire crackled. A couple of the counsellors were writing down lyrics to the songs the bunks were making up, planning to use them for Colour War later on.

"Does everyone always sing off-key around here?" a voice said behind them, and Jenna turned to see Blake standing next to Adam and Simon and wearing a look of slight annoyance on his face.

Karen saw him at the same time and froze mid-stanza, gave a little shriek of embarrassment, and dived for a marshmallow to hide her reddening cheeks.

"We sing however we want to," Alyssa said with a shrug.

Jenna smiled at that. Leave it to Alyssa to say whatever was on her mind. Jenna had always liked that about her, and she was relieved to see that Blake hadn't cast his spell on everyone...yet.

"That's the great thing about camp," Jenna said. "Nobody cares how bad we sound when we sing."

"Until now," Blake said, then broke into his easy smile, so that no one could be entirely sure whether he was insulting them or just kidding around.

"Wait until the final banquet," Nat said. "The whole

camp sings the Lakeview Camp alma mater so loud that the windows in the mess hall rattle."

Blake yawned indifferently. "Yeah, well, we'll see if I'm still around for the final banquet."

"What do you mean?" Tori asked. "*Everybody* goes to the final banquet. This year will be my first banquet ever, and I can't wait."

"Yeah," Adam said to Blake. "You'd miss out on all the great food and fun if you didn't go. Besides, the longer you stick around camp, the better chance you have of seeing some of Jenna's pranks."

"Pranks?" Blake repeated.

"Last year Jenna let all the animals out of the nature shack and into the mess hall at the camp dance," Adam explained. "She's the master prankster in these parts."

"*Retired* master prankster," Jenna corrected. "No more big pranks for me, not after Dr. Steve threatened to kick me out of camp."

"That's *so* my uncle." Blake rolled his eyes. "He just doesn't know how to have a good time. Which is why I'm giving this camp thing a trial run before I decide whether I want to stick around or not. I can call my dad's driver to come pick me up whenever I feel like it."

Jenna rolled her eyes and leaned over to whisper to

Nat. "How about he calls that driver right now?"

Just then, Simon walked over to Nat. "Is this seat taken?" he asked her.

Nat giggled. "It is now," she said, taking his hand as he sat down beside her.

Jenna sighed, scooting over to make more room for him. If Nat got any more cuddly with Simon, Jenna was going to lose her appetite. So she grabbed another marshmallow while she still had it.

Even though Nat was too lost in her own world to notice it, the next half-hour just confirmed for Jenna what she already thought was true. Blake sat down with Adam near Alex and Brynn, but he refused to roast any marshmallows or sing any songs. When Brynn told a spooky ghost story that gave Jenna chills and made her huddle closer to Alyssa and Perry, Blake just rolled his eyes.

"That was lame," he snorted, standing up from the fire. "I hate to break up the party, but I'm going to find my uncle and see if I can head back to the bunk. It's, like, two o'clock in the morning in Italy right now. I'm still on Lake Como time."

"You need to find Kenny, our counsellor, first," Adam told him. "He needs to know where we are at all times."

"Nah." Blake shrugged. "Uncle Steve's right over

there," he pointed to where Dr. Steve was helping supervise some of the younger campers roasting marshmallows. "He'll let me leave. No problem."

"Nothing like a little favouritism," Jenna said, watching as Blake talked to Dr. Steve and then wandered off towards the bunk alone. She couldn't believe Blake was getting special treatment from Dr. Steve, but at least he was gone for the night. That was a relief.

As counsellors started ushering campers off to the bunks, Jenna grinned at her friends. "Hey, I've got a fresh candy stash back in the bunk, if anyone's interested."

"You just ate five s'mores!" Chelsea gasped.

"Exactly." Jenna patted her stomach. "That leaves room for at least two of my mom's home-made brownies."

"Count me in!" Nat said.

"Me too!" Alyssa added.

"Will you allow a couple of campers from the bunk next door to crash the party?" Alex asked as she walked over with Brynn and Grace.

"As long as no one mentions boys for the rest of the night," Jenna said with a smile.

"Deal!" Alex said, and the rest of the girls chimed in.

"And as long as Andie and Mia say it's okay," Jenna

added. She looked at Mia and Andie expectantly, hoping they'd say yes.

"Give us a sec," Andie said, motioning Becky, the counsellor from 4C, over. The three girls talked, and then all nodded in agreement. "You guys can hang out in our bunk for a while, but you'll have to wait for half an hour before you come over," Andie said. "Because we're all assigning final electives now."

Alex and Brynn squealed with excitement, and Grace grinned. "That's worth waiting for," she said. "Besides, the casting list just got posted for the camp play. Becky said we could check it out before we go to the bunk. We're doing *Into the Woods* this year."

At the end of every summer, a big drama production was put on for all the campers on the night of the final banquet. Last year, the play had been *Peter Pan*, and Grace had played the best Wendy that Jenna had ever seen. Grace and Brynn both loved acting, and they were really great at it, too.

"I've never seen that play before," Jenna said.

Nat clapped her hands. "It's not a play. It's a musical, and I *love* it! It's the one that has all the fairy tales rolled into one show. That was one of the first shows my parents took me to see on Broadway." Nat and Tori were both in drama with Brynn and Grace, but Nat had decided not to audition for the show this year because, she said, she preferred acting serious drama parts instead of musicals.

"And I saw it when it came to LA," Tori said. She'd auditioned for the part of Little Red Riding Hood, and she was practically jumping up and down with excitement now, too. She turned to Andie. "Oh, Andie, can I please go look with them?"

Andie laughed. "Sure. Just be quick, okay?" she said, but Tori was already racing away with Grace and Brynn.

"So, I'll see you after we get our electives," Alex said to Jenna, heading towards her bunk. "Wish me good luck so I'll get sports."

"Good luck," Jenna called out. "To both of us!"

She waved goodbye, making a silent wish as she walked back to her own bunk that she and Alex would both get the electives they'd asked for.

Once everyone got settled back at the bunk and Tori reappeared, breathlessly exclaiming that she'd gotten the part of Little Red Riding Hood in the play, Andie took out her clipboard for the final elective assignments. Jenna and the other girls all rushed over to Andie, hovering over her to view their assignments.

"I won't be able to give them out if you suffocate me

first!" Andie laughed, but the girls were already looking for their names on the clipboard.

"Sports and boating," Jenna cried when she saw the electives next to her name. "Yes!"

"Are you ready to take on nature again?" Alyssa teased Nat as she looked at the clipboard.

"Not yet. I think I need until next year to mentally prepare myself for that," Nat said. Last year, Nat had nature as one of her first electives, but everyone knew that the closest she wanted to get to nature was painting her nails by the lake under a tree. "I got newspaper and drama."

"Um, Andie?" Tori asked hesitantly. "I know I already requested drama and art, but, um, do you happen to know what electives Blake signed up for? I thought maybe I'd be able to switch mine."

Andie shook her head. "Sorry, Tori. I don't think Blake's been given anything yet. Dr. Steve wanted to see how many empty spots were left in each elective before deciding where he might fit in."

"Oh." Tori's face fell, but then she brightened. "That's okay. Maybe he'll end up in my art class anyway."

"If he does, he probably won't want to touch the paints for fear of getting his Hugo Boss glasses dirty," Jenna said.

Just then, there was knock on the door, and Alex stuck her head around it. "Can we come in?"

"Yup," Andie said. "We just finished with electives."

"Us too!" Alex said, coming in with Brynn and Grace.

Jenna caught Alex's eye, and Alex gave her a thumbs-up sign and a big smile. That was all Jenna needed. She knew they had both gotten their first choice, and now they could play sports together for an extra hour every day.

"We have more big news," Brynn said with a grin after the girls had finished talking about who got what electives. "Grace and I got our parts for *Into the Woods*."

"And?" Nat asked expectantly.

Grace beamed. "I'm Cinderella."

"And I'm the witch!" Brynn said, raising her hands like claws and hissing in a villainous way.

"Congrats!" Jenna said. "You guys both get extra brownies and so does Tori, aka Little Red. The chocolate will help you all remember your lines."

"What?" Chelsea cried. "Since when does chocolate improve your memory?"

Jenna grinned. "As far as I know, there's not much that chocolate *doesn't* improve," she said, making everyone laugh.

As Jenna dug into her candy stash, she smiled and promised herself that nothing was ever going to distract her from her friends or from the soccer field and basketball court — particularly not some fancy schmancy guy from the Hamptons. Camp was almost over, and she was going to make the rest of her time here unforgettable.

CHAPTER TWO

Jenna sat on the sidelines of the newly mowed sports field and took a deep breath of the pine- and grass-scented air. These were the kinds of camp days she lived for. The sun was shining, there wasn't a cloud in the sky, and even though the air was already muggy and hot, it was still a perfect day for soccer. Jenna smiled as she pulled on her soccer shoes. In twenty minutes a bunk scrimmage between 4C and 4A would start, but Jenna and Alex had both gotten the okay from the counsellors to meet at the field early to practise and warm up.

Jenna pulled her hair into a ponytail to ward off the heat and was bending down to stretch when she heard Alex calling her name. She glanced up to see Alex walking towards her with Adam and Blake. Adam and Alex were walking comfortably close together and every once in a while their hands brushed against each other ever so slightly. But as soon as that happened, both of them would take a step away from each other, blushing shyly. Adam had this goofy grin on his face, and he kept sneaking side glances at Alex.

Oh brother. Jenna tried not to grimace, but there was something deeply disturbing about watching Adam attempt to flirt. Sure, she knew he'd liked Alex for a while last summer, too, but this summer was different. He seemed more serious about her this time. And there were just certain things a sister was never supposed to see her twin do, and flirting was one of them.

"Hey, Boo – er, I mean, Jenna," Adam corrected himself when Jenna cringed and threw him a dirty look. Boo was the nickname her family had given her when she was a baby, but Jenna hated it now that she was older. Of course, Adam still sometimes forgot not to call her that. "Alex told me you guys were playing, and I thought I'd take a few pictures for the newspaper before Blake and I head to free swim. And I just wanted to wish you luck." He ruffled her hair. "You'll need it." He broke into laughter, and Blake joined in.

Jenna fumed. Brothers could be such a pain sometimes. "Very funny, bro," Jenna said. "Just remember who wears the cleats in our family. I could run circles around you and your camera any day of the week."

Over the past two summers, Adam had turned into an amateur photographer. He tried to get photography as his elective as often as possible, but even when he didn't take it as an elective, he always had a camera strapped around his neck to take candid shots.

Blake laughed at Jenna's dig at Adam, and Jenna smiled at him. So he had a sense of humour. Well, that was a start.

"How was your first night at camp?" she asked, her smile growing wider as she watched him scratch a line of red bites on his arm. It looked as though the mosquitoes had worked their magic on him overnight. Maybe he'd try some bug spray now.

"Great," Blake said sarcastically, "for the bugs who made a home in the Waterford down pillows and comforter my mom shipped here in advance. I had to throw all of it out this morning and call my mother to send more."

"You threw them away?" Jenna cried. "We have a laundry room here, you know. Why didn't you just wash them?"

"Waterford is dry-clean only," Blake said dismissively, as if it were a fact that everyone in the universe knew, except Jenna. He shrugged. "It doesn't matter. My mom can have another FedExed here by tomorrow morning."

"They'll just get more bugs," Jenna said.

"We'll see," Blake said. "She's also sending a mosquito net...an unscented one. And some earplugs, too," he added. "Between Kenny's snoring and the chirping racket outside the window, I didn't sleep a wink."

"We call that chirping racket 'crickets'," Jenna said, giggling in spite of herself. This guy was unbelievable. Annoying, sure. Stuck-up, definitely. But Jenna was starting to find his tirades so ridiculous that they were actually funny. "Don't they have those in East Hampton?"

"Not on beachfront property," Blake said simply. "The only sound we have is the ocean waves, and I love that. I spend a couple of weeks every winter break in the Caymans with my dad and brothers on our yacht."

Alex's jaw dropped, and Jenna elbowed her to close it. She couldn't believe her ears. Was there anything that Blake didn't have?

She opened her mouth to say as much, but Adam gave her a warning with his eyes and jumped in with, "That's cool, Blake. Let's have a seat in the grass for a few minutes while Alex and Jenna warm up, okay? Then we'll head for the lake."

With that, Jenna kicked the ball into centre field, relieved that she didn't have to spend one more second around Blake, at least for now.

$$* \quad * \quad *$$

Jenna grinned at Alex as they passed the ball back and forth to each other, working their way towards the goal at the far end of the field. This was more like it. Just her, Alex, a soccer ball and a wide-open field. No boys to worry about, especially the annoying kind. Or so Jenna thought, until Alex suddenly asked, "What does Adam think of me?"

Jenna nearly tripped over the soccer ball but caught herself just in time. "Think?" she asked, giggling. "Adam doesn't think at all. Unless it's about food."

"Oh," Alex said, her face falling. "Okay, then. Forget I said anything."

Alex's mouth drooped a little more, and Jenna sighed. She wasn't used to having these kinds of talks. Nat and Tori were good at analysing guys, but she was much better at analysing soccer plays. And the last thing she wanted to do was talk to one of her best camp friends about her own brother. Eeeuw. She hadn't realized until now how Alex's little leftover crush from last year seemed to be growing by leaps and bounds.

"Listen," Jenna said. "Just because he hasn't mentioned anything to me doesn't mean he doesn't like you. I saw you guys talking to each other the other day,

31

and he looked really into it. And *hello*, he was here taking pictures of *you* today."

"Not just me," Alex said. "You too."

"Please." Jenna rolled her eyes. "He didn't come here to photograph his own sister."

"So maybe he thinks I'm cool," Alex said, almost more to herself than to Jenna. "That's good, right?"

Jenna nodded. "Yup. I think so."

"Cool." Alex grinned and gave the ball a strong kick straight into the goal. She motioned over her shoulder to where the girls from both bunks were walking towards the field. "So, what do you say we play some ball?"

"I thought you'd never ask," Jenna said.

Life didn't get much better than this. Jenna jumped into the air as she watched the ball soar towards the goal. Sarah, the appointed goalie that day for 4C, dived for the ball but missed by a centimetre or so. The ball sailed sweetly between the goalposts and fell against the net. Yes! Jenna did a victory dance for her third goal of the game.

"Great going, Jenna!" Andie and Mia yelled from the sidelines.

"Awesome!" Nat said, giving her a high five.

"Now all we need is a tiebreaker," Jenna said gleefully, checking the scoreboard as both teams headed to the sidelines for a half-time break. The score was 6–6. Alex was the big scorer for 4C, but she and Jenna were neck and neck, goal for goal. All Jenna had to do now was make sure her team could score again to win the game. The way her teammates were playing, though, that was going to be easier said than done. Sure, it was hot enough to fry an egg on the field right now, but that was no excuse for how 4A was performing out there.

For the first half of the game, Nat and Tori had been hanging back, afraid to touch the ball. Nat had gotten into kickball at the beginning of the summer, but was still pretty anti-sports at heart. Alyssa, Perry and Anna, though, had all been making a real effort. Alyssa had even scored two goals on her own, which was impressive, considering that she didn't usually get into sports that much either. But Lauren and Jessie had had to sit out for the rest of the first half after they both went for the same ball and knocked heads. Andie had assured Jessie that she showed no signs of a concussion, but Jessie was still worried about it. Jenna had glimpsed her sitting on the sidelines, first closing one eye and then the other to check if her vision was blurring. And Chelsea and Karen? Well, they were a disaster of an entirely different sort.

"I'm sorry I kicked the ball into the wrong goal," Karen apologized to Jenna for the hundredth time as they dug into the bag of orange slices that Mia had brought out to the field. It'd been so hot out the last few days, the counsellors had been providing oranges and water during sports so no one would get dehydrated – Dr. Steve's orders. Karen wiped a hand across her damp forehead and gave Jenna a worried look. "When you passed me the ball, I got so turned around, I totally forgot which side of the field our goal was on."

"Yeah," snipped Chelsea, "never mind that I was yelling the entire time that you were going the wrong way to try to get you to stop. I knew you were challenged in the coordination department, but I didn't know it was that bad."

Karen bit her lip, staring at the ground.

"Don't worry about it, Karen," Jenna said, giving her an encouraging pat on the shoulder. "You'll get it right in the next half. I know you will." Then she leaned towards her to whisper so only she could hear, "And if it makes you feel better, I saw Chelsea trip over her own shoelaces yesterday." She winked. "Miss Perfect has klutzy moments, too, just like everybody else."

Karen giggled. "Thanks, Jenna."

Jenna bit into another orange slice and sucked the

juice down first. Then she stuck the peel into her mouth to make a huge orange smiley face.

"A borange a bay beeps the boctor abay," she sang at the top of her lungs, as best as she could with the orange stuck in her mouth. Soon everyone was laughing, even Chelsea.

Jenna was in a great mood, even though her team had probably single-handedly set a record for Lakeview's funniest sports bloopers in just one scrimmage. Her bunkmates were in serious need of some training, but she was confident she could get them ready for Colour War, no problem. Even though not everyone in the bunk would be on the same team for Colour War, Jenna was playing it safe and trying to get everyone prepped so her colour team would be awesome, regardless of who was on it. With a few more scrimmages under their belts and some coaching tips here and there, they'd be ready for the sports competitions. But for today, Jenna was simply enjoying playing her heart out. She was playing forward, and she was on a rampage. Nothing could stop her. Except for maybe Alex. Jenna grabbed a second water bottle from the cooler, popped the lid, and shot a spray of water at Alex's back.

"Hey!" Alex cried, laughing. "Watch it!"

"Oops," Jenna said, faking surprise. "I'm so sorry."

"Very funny," Alex said. "But you'll pay for that on the field in the second half."

"I don't think so. One more goal, and 4C's going down," Jenna ribbed Alex good-naturedly. She was head-to-head with Alex, who'd scored the last three goals for 4C's team. But that was the way the two of them liked it. A little bit of friendly competition never hurt anyone.

"We'll see about that," Alex said. "I've been saving my best for last."

At the start of the second half, both teams took their positions on the field again, doing their best to ignore the sun beating down on them. When Mia blew the whistle, Jenna kicked the ball deep into the left corner of the field and watched as Sarah head-butted the ball to stop it, then passed it right up centre field to Tiernan.

Suddenly, Karen raced past Abby and Priya, who were trying to block her, and straight at Tiernan. Jenna couldn't believe it. Where had this aggressive side of Karen come from?

"Go, Karen!" Jenna screamed as Karen unbelievably stole the ball from Tiernan and began dribbling it down the field.

"Help help help help help," Karen was yelling as she ran. Now that she actually had the ball, she didn't have a clue what to do with it. Especially since Tiernan, after wiping the look of surprise off her face, had glued herself to Karen's side to try to get the ball back from her.

"Over here! I'm open!" Jenna yelled, waving her arms at Karen. "Kick it here!" Alex was on her like a hawk, trying to block her, but Jenna broke free and ran out into the open towards the goal. "Karen. Here!"

In a moment of panic as Tiernan, Abby and Priya all descended on her, Karen kicked the ball wildly up into the air. It headed towards Jenna, but she could tell it was going to land a few metres short. She shot into a sprint to see if she could reach it before Alex intercepted it.

She was running full force when her right foot seemed, strangely, to sink straight into the ground. Her leg twisted, her knees buckled, and a searing needle of pain shot up her calf. For a second, it seemed as if time stopped, and she was airborne. There was a flash of blue sky and green grass, and then she hit the ground so hard that her teeth rattled in her mouth. After that, there was nothing but the pain, the horrible pain, stabbing through her right leg.

*   *   *

"It hurts!" Jenna sobbed through clenched teeth, when she could breathe again.

"Jenna, are you okay?" a voice said close to her head. "Open your eyes and look at me. Please."

She felt two cool hands holding her head and brushing her hair and clumps of grass and dirt off her face. But she didn't want to open her eyes and look. No, it was better to keep them closed. Maybe if she kept them closed, her leg would stop throbbing as if it were being prodded by a thousand hot pokers.

"Jenna, please, come on, sweetie," the voice said. It was Andie's voice. Jenna recognized it now. "Open your eyes," Andie pleaded.

Jenna finally opened her eyes, letting the tears she'd been holding in run down her cheeks, and looked up into a sea of worried faces. "I think I'm okay," she whispered between sobs, wiping at her eyes. "My leg just hurts, but it'll be fine in a minute. I'll walk it off. What did I trip on?"

Mia scoped out the grass around where Jenna fell. "It's a groundhog hole," she said. "I think you just stepped right into it and tripped."

"Stupid groundhog," Jenna hissed as another stab of pain shot up her leg. "Stupid hole. I could've had that goal. I was wide open."

Nat, Alex and Alyssa gave weak laughs.

"Now I know you're going to live," Alex said, trying to kid. But Jenna could see the tears in her eyes, too. That made her cry even harder.

"Let's take a look at your leg," Andie said to Jenna. She reached to take off Jenna's shoe to check her ankle, but the second she got close to Jenna's foot, Jenna let out a howl.

"No! Don't touch it," Jenna said, her hands hovering protectively around her leg. Just the thought of the pain she'd feel if anyone touched it was enough to make her panic.

"Okay," Andie said, retreating. "No touching."

"Where does it hurt?" Alex asked, taking Jenna's hand.

She wiped away more tears and pointed to her calf. "Right along my shin."

"This doesn't look so good," Andie said. "Natalie, please go and get the nurse. And hurry."

"No!" Jenna said, trying to manoeuvre into a semi-standing position without putting any pressure on her right leg. She managed to get onto her left knee, with her right foot propped out in front of her, but even that little movement made her eyes water more. "I probably just bruised it when I fell or something," she said, in what she hoped was a convincing tone. "It's fine, really."

"Jenna!" Andie said sternly. "Lie back down. It could be broken!"

"I'm okay," Jenna said, ignoring her. She put all of her weight on her left foot and hopped around. But the second her right foot made contact with the ground, she sucked in her breath. "Yow!"

She let Andie and Mia put their arms around her shoulders and ease her back onto the ground, just as the nurse ran onto the field with Nat, a few of the counsellors, and – how embarrassing! – a stretcher.

"There's no way I'm getting on that thing!" Jenna said, pointing to the stretcher.

The nurse smiled sympathetically. "Let me just take a look first, and then we'll see, okay?" She gently examined Jenna's calf, touching it as lightly as she possibly could. A frown flickered briefly across her face when she rolled Jenna's sock down a bit.

"It's starting to swell," the nurse said, pulling out a huge pair of scissors.

"What are those for?" Karen asked, paling.

"I have to cut her shoe off," the nurse said. "If we don't get it off before her foot swells more, it could cut off circulation."

Jenna started to protest but then thought better of it. She didn't want her foot to fall off, that was for sure.

Alex grabbed her backpack from the sidelines and eased it under Jenna's head as a pillow while the nurse cut through Jenna's shoe and put a splint around her leg. Sarah gave Jenna some water and ibuprofen at the nurse's instruction, to help with the pain and the swelling.

"Do I get room service, too?" Jenna teased, trying to crack a smile for her friends.

"All right," the nurse said, standing up and motioning Andie, Mia and Kenny to bring the stretcher over. "We better get you to the infirmary and put an ice pack on your leg. Then you'll have to take a trip to the emergency room, I'm afraid. This has to be X-rayed."

Jenna's half-smile shrivelled up completely. "The emergency room!" she cried, and then she bit her to lip to turn off the waterworks she felt building up again. The last thing she wanted to do was spend the rest of this perfect day stuck indoors with a bunch of stuffy doctors, but one look at Andie's stubborn face, and she knew this was non-negotiable. That was when the panic set in. What if she had to have an operation or something? She tried to swallow her growing fear, not wanting anyone else to see it, but her heart was hammering so loudly, she was sure it was echoing for all to hear.

"I'll take you, Jenna," Andie said with finality, but then she leaned over and gave her a hug. "It'll be a quick trip," she said soothingly. "You'll see. But it's important to make sure your leg's not broken."

"Okay." Jenna finally nodded reluctantly. "Oh, the mortification," she said melodramatically as Kenny and the nurse carefully lifted her onto the stretcher. "Farewell, dear friends. I beg of you to forget this stretcher and remember me only in my days of glory on the soccer field."

"What are we going to do with you, Miss Jokester?" Andie sighed with exasperation, but she was smiling. Nat, Alex and Alyssa just shook their heads and smiled, too, but they still looked worried.

"I'll be fine," Jenna called back to her friends as she was carried off the field. "As long as no one else sees me on this stretcher." She smiled a little when she heard the sound of their laughter. That was her job, to make everyone laugh. But the last thing she felt like doing was laughing right now. All she could do, as the nurse led the way to the infirmary, was hope that things weren't as bad as they seemed.

CHAPTER THREE

Things weren't as bad as they seemed. They were worse. Jenna sighed and shifted in her emergency-room bed, replaying this afternoon's catastrophe over and over again in her head. Why hadn't she seen that stupid groundhog hole? Of all the ridiculous ways to end up in an ER, that had to be the dumbest. All of her earlier attempts to make light of this situation had fizzled out when she was faced with the creepily clean hospital. She couldn't even think of one single, solitary joke to tell to pass the time. More than that, she didn't even feel like joking. And when that happened, she knew she was in bad shape.

"Jenna?" A voice pulled her out of her thoughts. "Are you going to put down a card, or do I have to play your hand for you?"

Jenna blinked and looked up from the cards in her hand to see Andie sitting across from her on the bed.

"Sorry," Jenna said, trying to scratch at a spot on her calf hidden under the makeshift splint. "I guess I zoned out." She laughed half-heartedly. They'd been playing cards for the last three hours, in between filling out paperwork and waiting for doctors and nurses in the ER to come poke and prod Jenna. They'd made her put on a totally see-through hospital gown before they would X-ray her leg, and she'd been shivering ever since.

But that wasn't even the worst of it. The worst was that she'd been taken to the X-ray room in a wheelchair! How mortifying, when she could walk perfectly fine. Almost. Sort of. Okay...not really. She couldn't walk at all. And now she had to stay put in this bed – doctor's orders – until he came in with the results of her X-ray. If he *ever* came, that is.

Jenna sighed again, then handed her cards to Andie. "Can we take a break for a while? I don't feel like playing any more."

"Sure," Andie said. "How about a little celeb gossip instead?" She pulled *Cosmo Girl* and *US Weekly* out of her bag.

"Nah," Jenna said glumly.

"Your leg's not hurting you too much, is it?" Andie asked worriedly, tucking the blanket on the bed around Jenna's legs.

"Not too bad," she said. "I don't think anything's

broken." Maybe if she kept saying that, it would be true. Her leg was throbbing, even inside the splint, and every time she accidentally moved her toes or shifted her weight, the sharp pain was enough to make her eyes fill with tears all over again. She could tough this out... she *had* to. Colour War started next week, and she was going to play, no matter what. "I bet it'll be fine by tomorrow," she said hopefully.

"Maybe." Andie smiled sympathetically, and Jenna could tell she was trying (a little too hard) to stay optimistic. "Let's just see what the doctor says."

"Where is he, anyway?" Jenna grumbled. "They took the X-ray like an hour ago."

"About twenty minutes ago, to be more precise," the doctor said, walking into the room.

"Sorry," Jenna stammered, blushing.

"No apology necessary." The doctor smiled. "Waiting in an emergency room can make minutes feel like hours."

"You're telling me," Jenna agreed, smiling in relief.

"So, how's your leg feeling now?" the doctor asked, checking Jenna's toes and knee for swelling.

"Way better," Jenna lied. "I think we can take the splint off now. No problem. Nothing's broken, right?"

The doctor slid Jenna's X-ray out of a large envelope and clipped it onto a lit-up screen on the wall.

"Well, Jenna," he said, "it's not good news, but it's not as bad as it could've been, either. You have a hairline fracture in your tibia." He pointed to a very thin, barely perceptible crack on the X-ray of her calf bone.

"That means it's not broken, right?" Jenna asked, her heart giving a small leap of hope. "That means I can play sports again? If it's just a fracture."

"I'm afraid not," the doctor said gently. "A fracture is still a broken bone. You're lucky it wasn't a worse break. This type of fracture heals relatively quickly. But we'll have to set it, and you'll need a cast for about six weeks."

"Six weeks!" Jenna cried. "But that's for ever!"

"It'll go by faster than you think," the doctor said as he took down the X-ray, snapped Jenna's medical chart shut, and stepped towards the door. "I'll send for one of the nurses to apply your cast and show you how to use your crutches."

"Crutches, too?" Jenna flopped back on the bed as the doctor gave her one more patient smile before walking out of the room.

"The doctor was right," Andie said, squeezing Jenna's shoulder. "The next month will fly by. I broke my wrist when I was ten, and I had the cast off in no time."

"But you didn't break it at camp, right before Colour War, did you?" Jenna asked, not even trying to hide the crabbiness in her voice.

"No," Andie admitted reluctantly, "but you'll still have a blast in Colour War. You'll see!"

"Not in sports," Jenna said.

"You can be our token cheerleader!" Andie cried. But when Jenna shook her head, she tried again. "Mascot? Coach?"

"It won't be the same," Jenna whispered. She bit her lip, trying to fight back the tears. But she couldn't hold them back any more, even as the nurse wrapped the plaster cast around her leg. There went her chance to compete in Colour War. There went the rest of her summer...down the drain.

Just the sight of the Lakeview campground as they drove in from the hospital made Jenna feel even worse. As she looked out at the lake, which she wouldn't be swimming in, and the soccer fields, which she wouldn't be playing on, her heart took a plunge into the ground. She wobbled uncertainly on her crutches as she pulled herself out of the car, and she nearly tipped forward on her first awkward step. Luckily, Andie was there to steady her. Jenna didn't even have the energy to protest when Andie had to help her manoeuvre from the car to the bunk.

"Do you want me to see if I can get Pete to make a

plate for you from the mess hall?" Andie asked as they slowly climbed the few steps to the bunk.

"I'm not really hungry," Jenna said. Suddenly she felt exhausted. Her leg felt strangely heavy and clunky in its cast, and her armpits hurt from leaning on her crutches, even though she'd only been using them for a few minutes. Great. How were her arms going to feel tomorrow after a full day of crutching it? She didn't even want to think about it. All she wanted to do was crawl into her bed, pull the pillow over her head, and forget about this whole awful day.

But as she hobbled into the bunk, she saw that she wouldn't be getting her wish any time soon.

"Jenna!" Natalie cried, leaping off her bed and rushing towards her. "Are you okay? We've been so worried."

Alyssa, Tori, Karen and Jessie surrounded her, trying to give her half-hugs around the bulky crutches and help her to her bed all at once.

"So, what's the damage?" Alyssa said, inspecting Jenna's cast.

"A hairline fracture," Jenna said, making her best attempt at her usual carefree smile, but it wasn't easy. She had a feeling her friends could see through her, too.

As Jenna settled onto her bed, her friends flocked around her. Nat fluffed her pillows, Karen searched through Jenna's cubby for her pj top and a pair of shorts (since her pj bottoms wouldn't fit around her cast), and Mia broke out a set of permanent markers from the arts-and-crafts box under her bed.

"First things first," Mia said, sitting down at the foot of Jenna's bed. "Your cast is way too white. Don't you know white is out this season?" She flashed a rainbow of markers at the girls. "Leave it to us." She tapped the cast gently. "We'll make it so fabulous, we'll start a new fad. Castwear – for the truly trendy."

"I'm going to give Dr. Steve an update, and then I'll be back in a few," Andie said to Jenna. "I'm leaving you in good hands."

After she left, the girls crowded enthusiastically around Jenna's bed, picking colours for their artwork, and Jenna tried her best to put on a happy face. All the girls – even Chelsea (shocker!) – made a big show of signing her cast and rallying around her. But although Jenna appreciated their efforts, she still couldn't believe her bad luck.

Half an hour and ten permanent markers later, even Jenna had to admit that her cast looked more like a masterpiece than boring plaster. Alyssa had written a poem titled "Owed to a Groundhog" down the right side of the cast; Nat and Tori had painted soccer balls, basketballs and bunk cheers all over the rest of it; and all had signed their names and written encouraging messages.

"It looks great," Jenna said. "Thanks, guys."

Just then, Andie stuck her head around the bunk door. "I'm back, and I brought a few more reinforcements."

Adam walked in the door with Alex, Grace and Brynn.

"All right," Brynn said. "Let's see the war wound."

Jenna pointed to her brightly coloured cast.

Adam sat down on the edge of her bed. "Sorry about your leg, Boo," he said, ruffling her hair. "What a bummer."

"Tell me about it," Jenna grumbled. "And *don't* call me Boo."

"Right," Adam said. "Sorry."

Alex hugged her, then sat back to inspect her cast. "That's impressive," she said, looking for a place to sign it. "Too bad there's not a Colour War competition for cast crafts."

"No kidding," Jenna said. "With my crutches, I think the only thing I'll be able to compete in is Scrabble. And I *hate* Scrabble."

"Yeah," Chelsea said. "And you stink at it, too."

Alex rolled her eyes at Chelsea's remark, but only Jenna saw it. It made her smile.

"Colour War's not that big of a deal anyway, is it?" Tori said. "I mean, what's so special about it?"

"What's so special?" Jenna cried, throwing up her hands. "It's only the biggest event of the entire summer!" This was Tori's first year at camp, so Jenna couldn't exactly blame her for not understanding Colour War. But she needed to get filled in ASAP! "The whole camp gets involved in Colour War, and everyone – even people in the same bunk – gets divided into the Red and Blue teams. There's a huge rally and balloons and fireworks, and one year one of the counsellors even swung through the trees with red and blue torches," Jenna rambled, talking a mile a minute. "Then, the war's on. Every year the competitions are a little different. There're division events for separate ages and group events where everyone gets involved, and there're cheers and pranks and—"

"Whoa," Andie interrupted, laughing at Jenna. "Don't forget to breathe."

Jenna giggled and gulped in air. "Sorry...I *love* Colour War."

"Sounds...active," Tori said, actually looking a little frightened by the idea of spoiling one of her perfectly matched outfits. Only Tori and Nat would worry about something like that.

51

"It totally is!" Alex said, echoing Jenna's enthusiasm. She loved Colour War more than anything, too. "There's soccer, basketball, swimming, croquet, tug of war and Scrabble."

"Alex was the Scrabble champion last year," Adam said, shooting Alex a grin.

Alex's cheeks looked like two round strawberries for a few seconds, and she smiled shyly back at Adam. "And, um, then there's blob tag," she continued, "and one year we even had sumo pudding wrestling."

"It sounds really messy," Tori said. "But okay, I guess."

"It's more than okay," Jenna said. "It's fantastic! One of the best parts of camp."

Last year, she and Alex had been on the winning Blue team. They'd had so much fun together, even after Alex had to sit out during the soccer match because her blood sugar got too low. Colour War was one of the best memories she had of *every* summer. But now what did she have to look forward to?

She sighed. "I'm not going to be able to compete at all this year."

"Don't say that," Karen said. "We'll figure something out."

"Yeah," Nat agreed. "Nobody sits on the sidelines during Colour War, cast or no cast."

"I know you're not really into drama that much, but maybe you could play a part in *Into the Woods*, too," Grace said hopefully. "Just to give it a try. You might like it."

"There's a part with crutches?" Jenna asked doubtfully.

"You could be a tree," Grace offered, twirling one of her flame-coloured curls around her finger thoughtfully.

"A tree," Jenna repeated, deadpan. "*Great*. Nope, you're the actress, not me. I'd make a lousy tree. I wouldn't be able to remember all the lines." She tried to stifle a huge yawn, but it broke loose, and Andie picked up on it right away.

"Okay, it's way past curfew for all of you," Andie said with mock scolding in her voice. "Let our patient get some rest now."

"No," Jenna started to protest, but then she yawned again against her will, and Alex, Adam, Brynn and Grace waved goodbye while the other girls scattered around the room to get ready for bed. Jenna gladly let Andie help her slip into her pyjamas, and, with a sigh of relief, she crawled into bed. But trying to sleep on her side, like she normally did, wasn't too comfortable with the heavy cast on her leg. After a few minutes trying to get settled, she flopped onto her back and stared at the slats in the top bunk above her, listening to everyone

53

else's deep, peaceful breathing. She didn't know how long she lay there before drifting off to sleep, but when she finally did, she dreamed that she was sitting alone in her bunk, totally forgotten, as everyone else had a blast during Colour War.

CHAPTER FOUR

Jenna opened her eyes to see the sun shining in from the bunk's window the next morning, and she grinned. Another perfect day for soccer! She sat up in bed, feeling her adrenaline pumping already, and threw back her covers. And that's when the truth came crashing down on her, in the form of her new anvil-like cast. She remembered everything now – the groundhog hole, the emergency room, and the no-more-soccer doctor's orders. She frowned and gave her pillow a punch for good measure.

Then she weighed her options. She'd have to deal with her broken leg just like any good athlete would, that was all. Plenty of people in the world got around on crutches or in wheelchairs every day of their lives. She only had to endure it for six weeks.

She carefully swung her legs over the side of her bed and eased herself onto her crutches. So far, so good.

But she was the first one up, so she'd have to be quiet. Feeling like she'd grown two extra limbs overnight that she didn't know how to use, she cautiously took a few awkward lunges with her crutches, which got her a whopping metre away from her bed. Another metre, and another, and she'd almost made it halfway to the bathroom when Mia woke up and mass chaos broke loose in the bunk.

"Jenna!" Mia gasped. "Let me help you!"

Nat, Karen and Alyssa all leaped out of bed in record time and were at Jenna's side like three pyjama-clad musketeers, ready to rescue her.

"Take it easy," Karen said, putting her hand on Jenna's shoulder to steady her.

"I can walk to the bathroom, guys," Jenna said with a laugh. "Really. I'm not a total invalid."

The three girls took tentative steps back to let Jenna pass them, but they stayed within arm's reach, just in case.

When Jenna had safely made it to the bathroom door, she turned around and grinned. "If I'm not back in ten minutes, organize a search party," she teased.

She made it out in under three, instead, and took a little bow when she reappeared at the bathroom door.

"See?" she said. "I think I'm getting the hang of this. No problem."

*   *   *

Fifteen minutes later, and "no problem" had turned into "big problem". Jenna was half in, half out of the shower, trying to hang on to the slick tile wall while balancing her cast out behind her to keep it from getting wet. It had all been going so well...until she dropped her bar of soap on the floor. Now, she had shampoo in her eyes, she'd somehow managed to kick the bar of soap under the stall door with her one good foot (oh, the irony), and her towel had just fallen into a huge puddle on the floor.

She hopped out of the shower on her good foot, retrieved the now-drenched towel, wrapped it around herself, and stuck her head out of the stall.

"Hey, guys?" she called out. "Um, I think I might need a little help."

Nat was the first one on the scene, and she took one look at Jenna and burst out laughing.

"Hey!" Jenna protested. "Don't you know it's not nice to make fun of the shower-challenged?"

"I'm sorry," Nat said between more bursts of laughter. "It's just that you look like...like..."

"A drowned rat," Chelsea said, coming up behind her.

Andie walked in next, and after surveying the damage said, "Okay, we need a plan."

57

She and Mia went into action, and the next thing Jenna knew, she had a plastic garbage bag rubber banded around her cast, and she was showering in her bathing suit with Alyssa in the stall with her, helping her keep her cast out of the water.

Jenna sighed as Alyssa handed her the shampoo. Was there no end to this humiliation? Andie had already declared that Jenna would be the first one in the shower every morning, now that she needed the extra time. As it was, she and Alyssa were going to be late for breakfast this morning. But Andie said tomorrow would be easier, because Alyssa would be her shower buddy every day and help her get dressed afterwards. Of course, Jenna was glad that she hadn't gotten stuck with Chelsea as her helper, but that was beside the point. Lugging a mammoth cast around wasn't going to be quite as simple as she'd originally thought.

"Are you done?" Alyssa asked, holding out Jenna's towel.

"Definitely," Jenna said with a sigh. She was done with this whole day already, and it was only eight o'clock in the morning.

Jenna and Alyssa finally made it to the mess hall just as everyone else was finishing up their breakfasts, and Jenna dropped gratefully into her chair, since her crutches were already starting to make her arms ache.

Alex, Sarah, Grace and Brynn all waved to her from their table.

"How's the leg this morning?" Alex asked.

"Last time I checked, it was still broken," Jenna answered with a short laugh. "But it's not hurting as much in the cast any more."

Alex gave her an understanding smile. She'd been on crutches for a soccer injury during the school year.

"Hang in there."

"I'll get you some food, Jenna," Karen offered, standing up to follow Alyssa to the food line. As soon as they left, Andie sat down in the chair next to Jenna's.

"I know you picked sports as one of your final electives," Andie said to her. "But since you're not going to be able to play, I thought it might be good for you to pick an alternative. There were two extra spots in ceramics still open this morning. Would you be into giving that a try?"

Jenna's heart dropped, and she sighed. "But I don't know anything about pottery."

"You'll learn," Andie offered. "When I was a camper, I loved ceramics so much, I took it three years in a row. I still use the funky plates I made."

"Isn't there anything I can do outside instead?" Jenna asked. There had to be something she could do in the sunshine. It was bad enough to be stuck in this cast, but she didn't want to get stuck indoors all day, too.

"Well," Andie said, thinking, "your other elective was boating, but I'm worried that you might get your cast wet, so I think that's out, too. With all the other outdoor electives, you'd have to be able to get around on foot, which isn't going to work for you right now. I thought you might like taking art instead of boating."

"I guess I could do that," Jenna said reluctantly. At least she could sit outside and draw, even though her art skills had always been pretty pathetic.

"And then the ceramics instead of sports?" Andie tried again, but when Jenna didn't answer, she put her arm around her shoulder. "I know this is tough for you, but you've got to take it easy until your leg heals."

Nat jumped in with some encouraging words, too. "You could make some awesome jewellery in ceramics!" she said. "I saw this great article in *Teen Fashion* yesterday about DIY beading. It has instructions and everything. I was going to give it a try when I got back to New York, but I'll rip it out for you so that you can bring it to class with you. You can make some really fab stuff."

Jenna smiled at Nat's enthusiasm. Nat loved anything and everything having to do with fashion. "Well, if *you* say it's fab," she said, "I have to believe you."

"Trust her," Tori said. "I'm the expert on shoes, but she's the expert on accessorizing. She knows what she's talking about."

Jenna looked at all three of their expectant faces, waiting for her to make up her mind.

"All right," she said, trying to sound excited but failing miserably. "Ceramics it is."

Andie hugged her. "Great! You'll make some cool stuff, I'm sure."

Nat nodded in agreement. "When you become a rich and famous jewellery designer, I get dibs on a free pair of earrings."

"You might want to wait until you see how I do," Jenna said. "My jewellery may be too ugly to wear."

"Hey, ugly can be glamorous," Tori said. "It's all in the eyes of the wearer."

"You know," Andie said to Jenna, "we need some more people on the planning committee for the end-of-camp banquet, too. Do you want to be on the committee? You always have fun ideas, and staying busy would help take your mind off your leg."

"I do love the final banquet," Jenna said. In her mind, it was second only to Colour War. And if she couldn't participate in Colour War, at least she might be able to make the final banquet the best ever. "Okay," she said. "Sign me up."

"Great!" Andie said. "This is going to be terrific."

"Terrific," Jenna repeated. Yeah, right. More like boring. But she'd have to live with banquet planning, art and ceramics. Moulding clay wouldn't be nearly as much fun as scoring soccer goals, but — she had to face it — what other options were there for her and her plaster disaster of a leg? None.

Her mood didn't improve when, after lunch, she had to sit on the shore watching everyone else live it up during free swim. What good had it done her to learn how to dive last summer when now she wouldn't even be able to go in the water any more? She shifted on the blanket Andie had set up for her, wiped her hand across her forehead, and tried to scoot back further into the shade of the pine trees.

"Hold still, Jenna!" Tori scolded. "How can I buff your toenails if you keep squirming?"

"Sorry," Jenna said. "I'm just roasting. It must be forty degrees out today." She looked longingly out at the lake. Just yesterday she'd been doing cannonballs off the pier, relishing the cool water. But today she was stuck baking in the heat, watching everyone else swim. "I bet that water feels amazing."

"I wouldn't touch that water with a three-metre

pole, even with this heatwave," Nat said, glancing up from her mini-spa kit. She never went in the water during free swim – the lake algae creeped her out too much.

But Tori's hair was still wet from the last dip she'd taken into the lake. "The water's not that great," Tori said, but she looked guilty as soon as the words left her mouth.

"It's okay," Jenna said. "You don't have to lie about it. You should go get in again. I'm fine, really."

"And leave without finishing your pedicure?" Tori baulked. "That would be a violation of at least three big rules of pampering." She had willingly given up some of her swim time to give Jenna a manicure and pedicure with Nat.

"Now," Nat said, holding up three bottles of nail polish. "What'll it be? Pink Pout, Fab Fuchsia, or Sahara Sunshine?"

"Since I feel like I'm in a desert already," Jenna said, "let's go with Sahara Sunshine."

As Nat brushed on the first coat of polish, Jenna gazed out at the water. She could see Alex poised on the diving platform, while Sarah, Brynn, Valerie, Chelsea and Karen all watched, spellbound. Alex shot into the air in an impressive backward somersault, and as she hit the water, everyone burst into loud applause.

Even Nat and Tori put the spa session on hold for a minute to clap.

"That was incredible!" Sarah yelled in the water, sending a splash Alex's direction. "When did you learn how to do that?"

Alex shrugged. "I've never done it before," she said. "I just wanted to give it a try."

"No way!" Karen said with admiration.

Alex just grinned, and then she waved towards Jenna. "Hey, Jenna. Did you see that?"

Jenna forced herself to smile and nod. "Show-off!" she called out playfully, but then she realized that she felt there was a small grain of truth hidden in those words. Alex was looking every bit Miss Star Athlete, but she hadn't gotten out of the water once to come talk to Jenna and see how she was feeling. Even though Jenna knew that Alex had as much right to have fun as everybody else, she'd sort of expected her to be the one to give up swimming to hang out with her. It probably wasn't fair of her to get mad at Alex for not being able to read her mind. But still, they'd been friends for so long. Shouldn't Alex at least offer to sit with her for a while?

"Done!" Tori said proudly, holding out Jenna's hands for inspection. Jenna wiggled her toes, too, and Nat nodded in approval.

"A mani and pedi worthy of the best Manhattan salons," Nat said.

Jenna admired her sand-coloured fingernails and toes, then asked Tori to reach into her beach bag for her. "You're looking for chocolate," Jenna said, and when Tori pulled out two candy bars, Jenna nodded to her friends. "I can tip you with a Twix or a Snickers. Your choice."

Nat and Tori each took one, and then Tori pulled a pack of Twizzlers and Jenna's book from the bag for her. "Now," Jenna said, her tone all business, "if you ladies will excuse me, I have some serious reading to catch up on. And Tori, if you're not in that water in ten seconds, I'll throw you in myself."

Tori laughed. "I'd like to see that happen," she said, patting Jenna's cast.

"Go!" Jenna ordered, pointing to the water, and she could see Tori caving.

"All right, all right," Tori said. "But I'll be back to give you an intensive moisturizing hand treatment in fifteen."

Nat wiped her brow and stood up. "I think I'm going to sit on the pier to dip my feet in. Just to cool off."

"Tell me about it," said Jenna. "Enjoy the water, and don't worry, the lake's really not that toxic. You'll be fine."

Nat nodded. "But if anything, and I mean *anything*, slimy so much as touches my feet, I'm calling it quits."

Jenna looked on as Nat and Tori ran to the water, laughing all the way. Jenna sighed and buried her nose in her book. She didn't want to keep her friends from having fun, so she'd just suck it up and entertain herself for a while. She was reading *Little Women*, and at the moment she was feeling a special bond with the character Beth, the sickly sister who had to watch from her bed while everyone else rough-housed. Here she was, watching the summer slip away from the sidelines, too. *Poor Beth*, she thought. *Poor me.*

That afternoon, when she should've been at her sports elective, Jenna slowly hobbled to ceramics instead. To make things worse, she had to pass the soccer field along the way. There were Alex and Sarah, the two best athletes in 4C, shooting practice balls into the goal like pros.

"Hi, Jenna!" Alex shouted, giving her a wave. "We'll miss you out here today."

"I'll miss being out there!" Jenna called back. "Score one for me, okay?" She smiled. "Hey! Do you want to walk with me back to the bunks after I'm done at ceramics? Matt just sent me a new bumper sticker I want to show you."

Alex got a funny look on her face, then jogged over to Jenna. "I totally want to see the bumper sticker, but Sarah and I got special permission to stay on the field for an extra fifteen minutes for a longer practice. Adam said he might come by to take some more pictures for the newspaper." She dropped her eyes shyly to the ground. "So I'll be late for siesta. But maybe after dinner tonight, okay?"

"Sure," Jenna said, her smile drooping at the corners. "See you later."

The rest of the way to the ceramics shack, Jenna kept thinking about Alex...and Adam. She couldn't believe that Adam wanted to spend even more time with Alex. And that Alex seemed to want him to, too. That was the toughest part for Jenna. Alex had always been as anti-crush as Jenna was. But starting last summer and now even more this summer, that had all changed in a very weird way. And Jenna didn't like it. Not one bit.

When she finally hobbled into the crafts room ten minutes late, Farrah, the counsellor who taught the class, pointed to an empty chair. Jenna's eyes widened when she saw it, because sitting at her table was none other than Blake Wetherly, Dr. Steve's nephew. Blake liked ceramics? No way. It just wasn't possible. And it *certainly* wasn't possible that she would be able to endure sitting next to him every day.

Jenna sighed, took a deep breath, and made her way to the table. She thought about being nice and starting fresh with Blake, but when she opened her mouth to say hello, Blake beat her to the punch with, "So, I guess they thought you'd be better at Play-Doh than soccer, huh?" He snorted. "Well, at least if you're a klutz in here, you won't break anything, except maybe a ceramic mug."

Jenna's skin turned prickly hot with anger. "For your information, I'm *not* a klutz. It was a groundhog hole. I tripped. It could've happened to anyone." She stared him down. "And I didn't expect to see *you* here. Aren't you afraid of messing up your clothes?"

"Believe me, this wasn't my choice," he said. "This was the only elective they had room for me in, except for boating. And I'm taking that in the mornings." He looked around the room. "This is about as exciting as spending an afternoon with Martha Stewart. And I should know, because my parents are friends with her."

Jenna bit her lip to keep from completely losing it, and thankfully, Farrah started giving instructions. Jenna simmered down, but not enough. As soon as Farrah was done talking, Jenna picked up her ball of clay from the table and began pounding it. It gave her great satisfaction to imagine that she was really pounding Blake's stuck-up nose instead. She didn't know how long she pounded until she started feeling better.

"If you're trying to kill it," Blake said, smirking, "I think you succeeded about ten minutes ago."

Jenna blushed, but just pounded harder. "Well, I don't know what *you're* trying to make, but it looks like it could use some CPR, too."

"I don't care what it looks like," Blake said. "This class is totally lame anyway. The whole camp is."

"So why are you here then?" Jenna said.

Blake shrugged. "My parents made me come. They think hanging out here will make me 'well-rounded'." He rolled his eyes. "Whatever. This place is a dump. I'd rather be home with my iPod, chillin' by our pool."

Jenna shrugged. "Camp is really awesome. You should give it a try. If I were you, I'd be doing every activity I had the chance to. Trust me, it's better than being stuck with crutches. Especially with Colour War starting next week."

"Colour War sounds stupid, too. Who cares about the Purple and Pink teams?"

"Red and Blue teams," Jenna corrected, fuming.

"Whatever." Blake shrugged. "We'll see if I can spice things up around here, before we all die of boredom."

Before Jenna got a chance to ask what he meant, Farrah came over to check on their progress, and Jenna had to focus on moulding, instead of pounding, her clay into something resembling art. Or a coffee mug, at least.

"You should've heard him," Jenna vented about Blake as soon as everyone was together in the bunk that night. "Dissing camp like he was way too good for it. I can't believe Dr. Steve puts up with that."

"Maybe he doesn't know how bad it is," Karen offered.

Mia looked up from the horoscopes she was reading in *Cosmo Girl*. "Actually, you guys should try to be nice to Blake," she said. "Dr. Steve told Kenny that Blake's parents don't pay much attention to him. They're always going to parties and travelling, and Blake doesn't have too many friends his own age, except for ones that are probably even bigger snobs than he is. That's why Dr. Steve wanted him to come to camp for a couple of weeks this summer. Maybe Blake just doesn't know how to act around you guys yet."

"Oh, he knows how to act," Jenna said. "Like a *jerk*."

"Special delivery!" a voice called from outside, and Andie walked in, balancing two huge packages in her

70

hands. She laid the boxes down on Jenna's bed. "They came in the mail today."

Jenna checked the labels. "One's from my mom and one's from my dad." She ripped them open to find mounds and mounds of candy, cookies, Rice Krispies treats and a tub of gummy bears...yum. Both boxes were filled to the brim with sweets.

"Yes!" Jenna shouted gleefully. "Everybody...the candy's on me!" She grabbed a handful of candy bars and started passing them out.

"You keep eating all that junk, Jenna," Chelsea said, "and you'll gain so much weight you won't be able to play soccer even after your leg gets better."

"If you think it's junk," Jenna said. "I guess you don't want any, right?"

Chelsea froze, staring down at the Snickers bar in her hand. "Maybe 'junk' was the wrong word choice."

"You think?" Alyssa said, and everyone cracked up.

"There's enough candy here to stop world hunger," Anna said, splitting a huge Hershey's bar with Perry and Lauren.

"I guess I can't complain about my parents breaking up any more, because now I get double of everything!" Jenna grinned. "I have to admit, this is one benefit to having a broken leg." She thought about checking with Andie to see if she could ask Alex to come over to share the wealth, but then she remembered that Alex had promised to come see *her* tonight, and she'd never shown up after dinner. No, she wouldn't go looking for Alex. If Alex wanted to hang out with her, she knew where to find her.

CHAPTER FIVE

Dear Matt the Mad Scientist,

Thanks for the letter and the bumper sticker. I BRAKE
FOR BECKHAM — where did you find that, a soccer fan
website? And yes, I <u>do</u> get the play on the word "brake"
(smart alec). Believe me, it's not easy to forget my leg,
even though I'd love to. Every morning when I wake up,
I keep hoping the cast won't be there any more. But it
hasn't disappeared yet.

I know you say I should look on the bright side, but
so far that's been tough to do. I tried making a coffee
mug for Dad in ceramics, but yesterday when I took it
out of the kiln and filled it with water, the bottom fell
out. Go figure. Farrah, my ceramics teacher, says all I
have to do is find my niche, and I'll get the hang of it.
But I sure don't have the same skill with clay as I do in
sports. And there's this really annoying guy in my class,
too, who makes it impossible for me to concentrate.

I <u>hate</u> having to sit on the sidelines during sports every day (yawn — talk about boring!). I've been trying to coach my bunkmates to prep for Colour War, and I'm afraid it might be a lost cause (but don't tell them I said so). But — hey! — enough complaining.

I'd rather tell you about the weird stuff going on around here. First, you know my friend Alex? Well, I think she and Adam are crushing on each other again, just like last summer! Can you believe it? Of course, I don't know any details, and I soooo don't want to either. I'm still trying to get used to the idea of Adam hanging out with a girl without trying to impress her by burping the alphabet. Second, someone other than me has been playing pranks around camp! And believe it or not, Blake, the obnoxious boy in my ceramics class, was the first victim. Someone put a garter snake in his pillowcase last night. All I have to say is...justice has been served. He definitely had it coming to him. Of course, all the girls in my bunk thought I did it, because they know that I can't stand Blake. But then all I had to do was remind them that I couldn't sneak anywhere without clanging my crutches on the floor like a three-legged horse, and they believed me. But that leaves the question...who did it? At least I can keep myself entertained trying to figure that out, right? And, of course, thinking about

Blake and the snake and laughing...hard.

Gotta go. I have to try to coach our sorry soccer team now.

Write more soon!

Love

Jenna

"Come on, guys!" Jenna yelled from the sidelines, waving her right crutch in the air. "Keep your eyes open out there!" Even as she said it, she covered her own with her hand. This was getting too painful to watch. The game was going badly, and that was putting it mildly.

They were scrimmaging against 4C again, and they were losing...again. Jenna sighed. Alex was tearing up the field, playing better than Jenna'd ever seen her play. Sarah had switched positions from goalie to centre forward, and she and Alex were both scoring like crazy. Every time Alex scored a goal, Jenna felt a tightness build in her stomach. Why couldn't *she* be out there, too?

"Our bunk's getting better," Mia offered, setting up the water cooler on the grass. "You're doing a great job coaching."

Jenna shook her head. "No, I'm not," she said

glumly. "Nat just passed the ball to the other team by mistake. She practically gave Sarah that goal. Karen got hit in the stomach with the ball a while ago, and now she ducks every time it comes her way. Alex and Sarah look great out there, and we look like idiots."

"Nice coaching, Jenna," Chelsea yelled sarcastically from centre field as Alex scored another goal for 4C. "I thought you were supposed to be helping us play *better*, not *worse*. You don't have anything else to do, so what's the problem?"

"Ignore her," Mia said. "She's just frustrated. This hot weather is making everyone grumpy."

"Hey," Jenna said, examining the field more closely. "We lost a player. Where's Tori?"

Mia and Andie both scanned the field, but Jenna spotted Tori first. She was standing underneath one of the pine trees on the other side of the field, talking to Blake. Tori wasn't paying attention to anything happening in the game. Instead, she was laughing and chatting away with Blake in full flirt mode.

"What's *he* doing here?" Jenna cried.

"Good question," Andie said. "He's supposed to be in free swim right now." She took off towards them. "I'll be right back."

"Blake," Jenna heard Andie say, "you're ten minutes late for free swim."

Blake shrugged. "So? Uncle Steve doesn't care when I show up."

"Dr. Steve cares about all of his campers being on time for their activities," Andie said. "And that includes you."

He just rolled his eyes. "Whatever you say, *Mom*. I'm going, I'm going."

After he'd gone, Jenna caught up with Tori as she walked back onto the field. "What was that all about?" Jenna asked. "You're not supposed to leave the field in the middle of a game. You're supposed to work with everyone as a team."

Tori giggled. "Blake was just saying hi."

"Yeah, well," Jenna huffed. "Don't do it again. You're never going to start playing better if you don't practise."

Tori frowned as she joined everyone else. "It's just a game, Jenna. Relax already."

But Jenna couldn't relax, especially when, at half-time, Alex and Sarah started in with some razzing cheers.

"4C rules, and we all know it,
We're kicking butt today to show it.
We're soccer queens, better than the rest,
You're gonna lose, 'cause we're the best."
Alex hooted and gave Sarah a high five.

"Give it a rest, will you?" Jenna said to Alex. "We know we're losing. We don't need to be reminded with your stupid cheers."

"Don't be mad, Jenna," Alex said. "It's all in good fun. We always used to razz each other about stuff like this before you hurt your leg."

Jenna sighed. "You're right. I'm sorry."

Alex grinned. "No problem. You're not as sorry as you will be when we win." She gave Jenna a friendly slug on the shoulder.

"Ha-ha," Jenna said, trying to smile as Alex and Sarah headed out onto the field again.

"Don't pay attention to them," Jenna told her team. "We can still beat them."

"I don't think so, Jenna," Nat said. "It's so hot, I can barely breathe. I'm exhausted."

"Me too," Perry said.

"Count me in for three," Anna said.

"Come on!" Jenna said, mustering up an encouraging smile. "You can do this!"

She turned to Alex, Sarah, Brynn and the other 4C players, and cheered:

"You may think that you're the best,
But we're going to put that to the test.
We'll make you pay with every play,
You'll need crutches, too, by the end of this day!"

"That was...forceful," Andie said when Jenna finished, out of breath. But Alex and Sarah just cracked up laughing, which made Jenna even madder.

"Listen," Jenna said, leaning towards her teammates. "You get out there and start playing, or none of you will stand a chance in Colour War, no matter which team you're on."

"Thanks for the vote of confidence," Alyssa said, shaking her head and slowly heading back onto the field. No one else said one word. They just took their positions on the field and played even worse than before.

After a final score of 20–3, with 4C reigning victorious, Jenna headed to lunch in a foul mood. She definitely didn't feel like being social, and she wasn't feeling much better during the bunk's siesta time that afternoon. Everyone else was being ultra-careful around her, as if they didn't know what might set her off into grumpy mode again.

"Okay," Andie said, pulling out her *Cosmo Girl*. "Who wants to take the 'What Would You Do for a Million Dollars' quiz?"

"I'm in!" Nat said.

"Me too!" Chelsea, Karen, Perry, Laura and everyone else echoed.

"I'll be right there!" Tori yelled from the bathroom. "I'm just brushing my teeth. I can't get the disgusting taste of those fish sticks we had for lunch out of my mouth."

"Jenna," Mia said, handing out sheets of flowered stationery to everyone to write on, "do you want to take the quiz, too?"

"Nah," she said, holding up her copy of *Little Women*. "I think I'll read instead. I'm getting really into this. Beth's my favourite character."

"Oh, that's a smart pick," Chelsea said. "She's the one who kicks the bucket."

"Chelsea!" Jessie said. "Don't give away the story."

"That's okay. I knew it was coming anyway," Jenna lied. Then she stared at the pages of her book. How depressing. Well, Chelsea had just put a damper on her plans for afternoon reading. She forced herself to keep turning pages, though, so that no one would bug her as the quiz started.

"What would you do for a million dollars?" Andie asked, reading from the magazine. "Would you rather eat a bucket of worms or show up naked to school for a whole week?"

"Worms," Nat said decisively. "There's no *way* I'd get caught naked at school. That's my worst nightmare."

80

Tori walked out of the bathroom with her toothbrush in her mouth.

"I know what I'd do for a million dollars. Or maybe just for a dollar." She grinned. "Kiss Blake Wetherly."

"Eeeuw!" Chelsea squealed.

"What?" Tori said, looking hurt. "I know he's a snob, but he's a cute snob."

"It's not that," Lauren said, her eyes widening. "It's your...your teeth!"

Tori's hand flew to her mouth. "What's wrong with them?"

"They're purple!" Alyssa said, rushing over to Tori. "Your whole mouth is purple!"

Tori screamed and ran for the bathroom, with everyone else following behind. Jenna took an extra long time to get to the bathroom door, but when she finally did, she saw Tori bent over the sink, frantically washing her mouth out with water, while Andie inspected Tori's toothpaste.

"It looks like purple food colouring," Andie said. "Someone must have filled your toothpaste tube with it."

"Why didn't I look before I stuck my toothbrush in my mouth? Why? Why?" Tori shrieked. "Will it come out? What should I do? I can't leave the cabin looking like this."

Jenna stifled a giggle. Tori looked a little like she was turning into a grape from the inside out. Her lips were bright purple, and when she opened her mouth, her teeth were even worse.

"Keep rinsing with water," Andie instructed her.

"The mystery prankster strikes again, huh?" Jenna said.

As soon as she said it, Andie, Mia and all the girls turned, in unison, to look at her.

"What?" Jenna asked.

"Jenna, can I talk to you for a minute?" Mia asked, leading her out of the bathroom. When they were out of earshot from the other girls, Mia said, "I know you have a tradition of playing initiation pranks on new campers. You've been very good so far this summer, though, so I don't have any reason to believe that you would do this. But...should I?"

"No! Of course not." Jenna grimaced. She'd been accused of pulling pranks before when she was innocent, especially when Gaby, Chelsea, or the guys from Adam's bunk planned something, but why did everyone *always* have to suspect her first?

"Good." Mia sighed. "I'm sorry I asked, but sometimes it's hard to break old habits. I'm just glad to hear that you had nothing to do with this. Do you have any idea who did, though?"

82

"Nope," Jenna said. "Not even one clue." And it was true. "But you have to admit it was funny."

Mia just shook her head, a tiny smile playing at the corners of her mouth. "Maybe," she admitted. "But Tori isn't laughing." She sighed. "Come on, let's help her get cleaned up."

Tori's teeth still had a slightly grape-ish tint to them at dinner time, but luckily, no one else outside of their bunk noticed. Jenna, though, had definitely noticed a couple of suspicious glances Tori had given *her*, and it seemed like Nat and Alyssa were looking at her with a big question in their eyes, too. The fact of the matter was, regardless of what anyone was saying out loud, Jenna was being treated like the primary suspect for the pranking. And she hadn't even done anything!

She was almost relieved when, after dinner, she got to escape the bunk for a little while to go to the first banquet committee meeting. No one else from her bunk was on the committee, but she was glad to see Sarah and Tiernan from 4C when she walked through the door. They waved her over to a chair where she'd have enough room to stretch out her leg.

"Thanks for saving me a seat," she said.

"No problem," Sarah said. "We heard about the

prank you played on Blake the other day with the snake in the bed. That was genius. You deserve the best seat in the house for sticking it to that preppy boy."

"But...that wasn't me," Jenna stammered.

"Sure it wasn't." Tiernan winked. "No worries. Your secret's safe with us."

Jenna started to protest again, but just then Dr. Steve called the meeting to order. Once it started, Jenna remembered why, as much as she loved the final banquet, planning it had never been something she'd been interested in. First, none of the campers could agree on a food choice. Then, no one could agree on decorations. Finally, everyone gave up trying to agree altogether and just started arguing among one another.

"Simmer down, ladies and gentlemen," Dr. Steve said calmly. "No need to throw the camper out with the bug juice."

"Huh?" Tiernan whispered.

"That's Dr. Steve lingo for let's not get ahead of ourselves," Jenna interpreted. Dr. Steve was always using strange camp expressions that even she sometimes had a hard time figuring out.

"What we need is a theme first," Dr. Steve explained, "and that will help us pick the music, food and decorations."

"How about a baseball theme?" Sarah said. "Hot dogs, French fries, and 'Take Me Out to the Ball Game'."

"How about a fairy tea party?" one of the third-year girls suggested timidly, her eyes twinkling. "We could all make crowns to wear and paint unicorns on posters and sprinkle sparkly fairy dust all over the tables."

"Those are both good ideas," Dr. Steve said encouragingly. "Let's keep thinking so we have a variety to choose from."

Ten minutes of brainstorming brought ideas for everything: from country hoedowns (too much like last summer's square dance) to Mexican fiestas (too spicy) to masked balls (too fancy). Even Dr. Steve was starting to look a little weary, when Jenna hit on the perfect idea.

"What about an Italian feast?" she said. "We could put red-and-white-chequered tablecloths on all the tables, and candles, too. And we could have spaghetti and meatballs, and chicken parmesan, and—"

"Garlic bread," Sarah jumped in, getting excited.

"We could even decorate a couple of the canoes to be like the gondolas they have in Venice," Tiernan suggested.

Dr. Steve smiled, and soon all the kids were coming up with ideas for drinking grape juice out of plastic goblets, building a Leaning Tower of Pizza, and a make-your-own gelato station.

"Could there be Italian fairies?" the third-year girl asked, making everyone smile.

"We'll see," Dr. Steve said. "But it sounds like we might have a banquet theme. All in favour of an Italian feast, raise your hand."

A sea of hands shot into the air.

"Then it's decided," Dr. Steve said. "The counsellors and I will get the supplies, and at the next planning meeting, we'll get started on the decorations. And a big thank you goes to Jenna Bloom for coming up with such a terrific idea."

Jenna smiled and blushed. For the first time since her accident on the soccer field, she really felt good. Maybe Andie had been right. Being on the banquet committee would help her take her mind off her leg. And now she could make sure it was the best banquet ever.

As she was pulling herself up onto her crutches to leave, she caught sight of Adam standing in the far corner of the mess hall, his camera to his face.

"Hey, Adam." She waved. "What are you doing here?"

Adam put his camera away and walked over. "Dr. Steve asked me to take some photos for the newspaper."

"Do me a favour," Jenna said. "Don't take any of me in my cast. It's something I'd rather forget."

"Okay, no cast pictures in the paper," Adam said. "But you have to do something for me, too." He suddenly went from looking like his normal, stinky, teasing, brotherly self to looking shy.

"I can't believe it!" Jenna laughed. "Are you actually blushing? What could you need that makes you look that ridiculous?"

Adam turned even redder. He reached into his camera bag and pulled out a yellow envelope. "Look, this is totally not a big deal, but...would you give this to Alex? Next time you see her, I mean?" He stared at the ground. "It's a photo I took of her on the soccer field. It's going to be in the last camp paper. But I thought she might like a copy, too."

Jenna groaned inwardly. A photo was like Adam's version of a love letter...gross! And now he wanted *her* to deliver it? Had she suddenly grown wings and a bow and arrow? Playing cupid to her brother and one of her best friends...this was getting *way* too weird. But then she looked at her brother, who was still blushing furiously. How could she say no?

Jenna peeked into the envelope. There was Alex, running full force with the ball speeding along in front of her, her short hair fluttering behind her, a huge smile

87

on her face. The photo captured exactly how Alex looked on the soccer field, and you could see from her face how much she enjoyed it.

"This is good, Adam," Jenna said softly. "Really good."

"Yeah, well, will you give it to her?" Adam said.

"Sure." Jenna nodded. "She'll love it." She didn't want to tell Adam that things had been a little awkward between her and Alex lately. Maybe she'd feel better about things tomorrow, and she'd give her the photo then.

"Thanks, sis," Adam said.

As they walked out of the mess hall together, Jenna thought about the photo with a tiny pang of sadness. If she hadn't broken her leg, that happy smile would have been on her own face, too, as she kicked the soccer ball straight into the goal.

Jenna had just slid the photo into her cubbyhole and grabbed her pjs to get ready for bed when she heard the bunk door slam. She looked up to see Alex standing in front of her, wearing a very strange tie-dyed T-shirt two sizes too big for her small frame and holding a bundle of clothes in her arms.

"All right, Miss Jokester," Alex said with an

exasperated expression that seemed to be debating between laughing and frowning. "This is all very funny. I don't even know how you pulled it off with your leg. But where are they?"

"What?" Jenna asked blankly.

"My clothes!" Alex blurted out. "They're all gone. They disappeared from my cubby and were replaced with these." She held up the bundle of clothes. "Guy's clothes. Whose...I don't know."

"I didn't do anything with your clothes," Jenna said. "Honest." She looked at the clothes in Alex's arms. "Wait a minute...those look like—"

Adam's clothes, she was about to finish just as Adam himself walked into the bunk, wearing one of Kenny's counsellor T-shirts and a very baggy pair of shorts.

"Jenna, what did you do with my clothes?" Adam started, then froze when he saw Alex. Adam looked from the bundle of clothes he had in his arms to the bundle Alex had in hers.

"My clothes!" they both said at the same time. Then they took turns blushing and mumbling awkward apologies as they switched all of their clothes.

"I'm sorry, guys," Jenna said. "But I didn't have anything to do with this. Really."

"Yeah, sure," Adam said. "I know one of your pranks when I see it. And I also know that you've got way too much free time on your hands now that you can't play soccer. Funny coincidence, isn't it? You break your leg, and all of a sudden pranks start happening all over camp. It doesn't take a genius to figure that one out."

"But, but—" Jenna stammered, but Adam wouldn't hear it.

Once he had his own clothes back, he shot Jenna a dirty look and left the bunk with a still-scarlet face.

After he left, Alex turned to Jenna with a glare. "Thanks for totally embarrassing me," she whispered. "I can't believe you'd do that to me, especially when you know that me and Adam...that I..." Her voice died away. "Adam will never talk to me again, thanks to you."

"Alex, please believe me," Jenna said. "I wish I knew who did this, but I don't. You're taking this way too seriously. It was just a prank."

Alex bit her lip, and tears welled up in her eyes. "A prank that was meant to humiliate me in front of the guy I like. Who would've known that except you?" She wiped her eyes. "I thought I could trust you. But now I know better." She walked out without another word.

Jenna looked around at her bunkmates, who seemed to be frozen over their magazines and letter-writing, all staring at her.

"Doesn't anyone believe me?" Jenna asked, throwing up her hands.

"Hey," Alyssa said, "if you say it wasn't you, then it wasn't."

"Yeah," Nat said, and the other girls nodded in agreement, but there was doubt in their eyes. Luckily, Andie and Mia were both out at a counsellor meeting, so they'd missed the whole episode. Otherwise, Jenna would've had to endure way more than questioning eyes. At least she was grateful that it was only her bunkmates who knew about this so far.

But as Jenna got ready for bed, she couldn't help feeling that her friends didn't trust her, either. And she didn't have a clue how to convince them otherwise.

CHAPTER SIX

The next morning, someone pounding on the door woke everyone in bunk 4A bright and early.

Jenna and the other girls opened bleary eyes to see Becky, the counsellor from 4C, standing at the door.

"Can I talk to you guys for a minute?" Becky asked Andie and Mia.

The three of them whispered back and forth for a few minutes, and then all three pairs of eyes focused on Jenna, who was just then groggily sitting up in bed.

"What?" she asked, stifling a yawn. "Don't tell me Adam broke *his* leg or something."

"Jenna," Andie said, "did you leave the mess hall during dinner last night? Or make any stops on your way back here from the banquet planning meeting?"

Jenna shook her head. "Is this about Alex's and Adam's clothes?" she said, panicking. "Because I already told them, that wasn't me."

Becky and Andie looked at her blankly. "What happened?" Becky asked. "Alex didn't mention anything to me about it."

"Oh," Jenna said, relieved that Alex hadn't run straight to Becky to blame her for last night's clothing switch. "Never mind. Everything's fine now."

"Not really," Andie said. "Last night someone stole all of 4C's pillows and stuffed the pillowcases with rice. No one realized it until they were crawling into bed."

Jenna resisted the urge to laugh as she pictured Brynn, Alex, Sarah and the other 4C-ers tossing and turning on mounds of rice all night long. A smile snuck across her face before she could stop it. "That must've been quite a night," she said.

"The girls spent half the night trying to clean the rice out of their beds," Becky said, "and the other half searching for the pillows, which *still* haven't turned up."

Andie turned to Jenna. "Between the prank played on Blake earlier this week, the one on Tori, and this, I don't know what to think. Did you have anything to do with this, Jenna?"

"No way," Jenna said firmly. Why was it that everyone was blaming her for things these days? "Come on, you guys," she tried again. "I've been supergood this summer. I've barely played any pranks. Plus, I played that rice trick on Adam's bunk two summers ago, and I *never* repeat a prank."

Andie sighed. "We're going to give you the benefit of the doubt," she said, "and believe you. But hopefully this type of stuff won't keep happening. And if it does, Jenna, I seriously hope you're telling the truth, and that you're not involved. Because if you are, it's going to mean trouble."

Jenna nodded. She was at a total loss. Not only was she stuck in this awful cast for the most fun part of camp, but now everyone was turning against her. No one was saying out loud that the pranks were her fault, but she could feel them blaming her. Her own friends didn't trust her any more, and that hurt more than anything.

Things didn't get any better during sports later that morning, either. Everyone from 4A and 4C was keeping a safe distance from Jenna. It was almost as if they were keeping a staunch lookout, waiting for her to pull another prank.

Jenna did her best to ignore the sinking feeling in her stomach as the girls warmed up for their scrimmage, but she was getting more frustrated by the second. When she saw Alex and Sarah walk onto the field, Jenna figured that now was the chance to try to make everything okay again. She'd even brought Adam's photo along to give to Alex. Alex would never stay mad at her when she saw the photo Adam had taken of her.

"Hey, Alex," Jenna waved to her and gave her a friendly smile. She reached into her sports bag to pull out the photo.

But before Jenna could explain what was in the envelope, Alex frowned and said, "Thanks for keeping us up all night, Jenna. That was really great of you. Especially after stealing my clothes, too."

Jenna stared down at the envelope in her hands, thinking of the photo inside. She shoved it back into her bag. Fine. If Alex didn't trust her any more, why should Jenna stick her neck out for her? Forget it. Being the go-between for Alex and Adam was weird enough as it was. She didn't owe them anything, especially after being treated like this.

"All right, you guys!" she yelled at the 4As, who were taking their places on the field. "Today's the day we kill 4C!"

By the end of the second half, they weren't killing. They were *being* killed. And Jenna had never been so furious with her friends. 4C was playing better than ever. With Alex and Sarah together on the team, they were proving unbeatable. Alex and Sarah were on fire, scoring goal after goal. And every time Alex scored, she made a big show of whooping and high-fiving. Jenna was starting to feel as if each goal was meant as a little dig at her, and she couldn't stand to see Alex gloating any more.

"Nat!" Jenna screamed from the sidelines when Nat, who had the bad luck of playing 4A's goalie this game, missed another ball. "Are you blind? Why didn't you catch that?" She knew she was not being the most patient, or understanding, coach in the world at this moment. But this was ridiculous. She was sick of feeling as if no one on her team except for her cared about sports. And she was *really* sick of having to watch from the sidelines while everyone else played so horribly.

Nat picked herself up off the ground after dodging from the ball. "That ball was going, like, fifty miles an hour!" Nat said. "I value my life. There was no way I was sticking my face in front of that missile."

"That's the fifth one you missed!" Jenna shouted, throwing one of her crutches onto the ground. "Get it together out there!"

Nat nodded and bit her lip, and a few seconds later, Jenna saw her wiping her eyes.

"Oh, are you crying now?" Jenna yelled. "Suck it up!"

"Jenna," Andie said, coming up beside her. "Let's take a break for a minute and cool off, okay?"

Andie called a time out, and Nat, Alyssa, Karen and the other 4As dragged themselves off the field, dirty, sweaty and frowning.

"If you keep playing like this," Jenna told them, "you're going to be dead meat in Colour War."

"It's forty degrees out there," Perry said. "This heat is unbelievable."

Nat nodded in agreement. "Simon's meeting me after this to walk me to art, and I'm completely sweaty. He's going to be so grossed out." She sighed. "Sorry, Jenna, but we're doing the best we can."

"Yeah, ease up, Jen," Alyssa said. "It's just a practice game."

"But that's the whole problem," Jenna said. "No one's taking this seriously."

"Hello!" Chelsea said. "When did you become the Soccer Dictator? Get a grip."

"You just don't get it," Jenna said. "None of you know the first thing about playing sports."

Jenna sank down in the grass on the sidelines as play started again. It was no use. She might as well give up trying to coach her friends. They stank at sports, and there was no way she could teach them how to play in time for Colour War. In fact, she was hoping now that she wouldn't be on the same colour team as any of her friends – not at the rate they were botching sports. She was miserable, wanting more than anything to be out there on the field, to have her leg miraculously healed so that she could get her game, and her smile, back. It was so hard to feel this helpless, and so disappointing to know she couldn't help her friends more. But the sadder she felt on the inside, the angrier she got on the outside. She didn't like the Jenna that was yelling at her friends, but at the same time, she couldn't stop her, either. She watched the rest of the game half-heartedly, and when 4C scored their final, winning goal, she didn't get in line to shake hands with them or tell them they'd played a good game.

She just sat there as the players put their equipment away, staring glumly at Alex and Sarah picking up the soccer balls from the field.

Alex kicked the last of the soccer balls straight into the net, then did a victory dance on the field and high-fived Sarah.

"That's the best shot I've ever made," she said to Sarah, beaming as the two of them walked off the field towards Jenna.

"It was awesome," Sarah said.

"Take a chill pill, Alex," Jenna said coolly. "It wasn't that special. I could've made that shot with my eyes closed."

Alex frowned. "You know what? I'm sick of this poor-me attitude you've got, Jenna. You're pulling pranks again to get attention, just because you're bored and you can't play sports with the rest of us any more. But I never thought you'd lie to me about anything. You lied to me about switching my clothes around, and you're lying about the rice, too. Everyone knows it was you. And I'm proud of the way I played today. I deserve to celebrate. And I don't care whether it bothers you or not."

"Yeah, well, I'm sure if Adam saw your ridiculous victory dance, it'd bother *him*," Jenna said. She hated the awful words she was saying, but she couldn't stop them. "And he definitely wouldn't think you were that special, either." Just as Alex's face crumpled into tears, Jenna turned and left, as fast as her crutches could carry her.

"Jenna, wait up!" a voice called behind her.

But Jenna didn't want to wait. She willed her crutches to move faster, until her legs were swinging so high with each step that she slid on some loose gravel, nearly toppling backwards.

"Whoa," Adam said, grabbing Jenna's shoulders to steady her. "I've never seen anyone on crutches move that fast before."

"I'm hungry." Jenna shrugged, not wanting to get into the real reason why she had left the soccer field in such a hurry.

"Well, hold up a minute. I was hoping to catch you at the sports field, but Alex said you'd already left. I wanted to talk to you—"

Jenna cut him off. "Before you say anything else...it wasn't me."

"What wasn't?" Adam asked.

"Whatever it is you're coming to blame me for," Jenna said.

"I'm not coming to blame you for anything *new*," Adam said. "But I am still mad at you for the clothing switch last night." He gave her a half-playful, half-serious slug on the arm. "What was up with that?"

Jenna put her head in her hands. "How many times do I have to say it?" she cried. "I didn't do it!"

Adam held up his hands. "Okay, okay. That look in your eyes is almost enough to scare me." He snorted. "Almost."

"Adam, before you force me to hurt you," Jenna glared at him, "which I *will* do...what do you want?"

Adam suddenly went quiet and dug his shoe into the dirt. "I was just wondering if...if you gave that photo to Alex yet," he mumbled, staring at the ground.

Jenna stalled. Now what was she supposed to say?

She couldn't tell him that she was in the middle of a big fight with Alex without unleashing enough questions for the Spanish Inquisition. And there was no way she was going to give Adam's photo to Alex now, not with the way she'd been acting. After all these years of friendship, Alex didn't even know her well enough to believe she was innocent of the pranking, so why should Jenna go out of her way to do something nice for her? No way. She was tired of the two of them asking for her help and even tired of them liking each other. The sooner Adam lost interest in Alex, the better. So instead of telling Adam that she hadn't given the picture to Alex yet, Jenna did the only other thing she could think of. She lied.

"Sure, I gave it to her yesterday," she said. "No biggie."

"But...did she say anything?" Adam asked. "Did she like it?"

She shrugged. "I have no idea. She didn't open the envelope in front of me."

"Did you tell her it was from me?" Adam asked.

Jenna nodded, feeling guiltier by the second. "Sure, and she said she'd look at it later when she had time."

"Oh," Adam said, his face falling in the tiniest way that only Jenna could pick up on. "Okay." Then he smiled, and Jenna could see him forcing it to stay on his face. "Well, I've gotta catch up with the other guys. I'll catch you later."

"See ya," Jenna said, watching him go as her conscience settled in to give her a nice long lecture. Well, she'd hit a new low. Lying to her brother was something she'd never done before, and even though she felt a small satisfaction in knowing that she'd sabotaged Alex's chances with Adam, she also felt a nagging guilt. As she made her way into the mess hall, she wished she could forget what she'd just done. But somehow, she knew she was going to have a hard time thinking about anything else.

She was still thinking about it, with a tightness in her stomach, when Andie got in the food line next to her.

"I heard you and Alex fighting earlier on the soccer field," Andie said. "It's not like you two to fight. What's going on?"

"Nothing," Jenna mumbled. "I just wasn't in the mood to hear her gloating over the game."

Andie helped her get a plate of ravioli, which actually smelled semi-edible for a change, and picked up both her tray and Jenna's to lead the way to the bunk's table. "Jenna, hold up a minute," she said, motioning her to a quiet corner of the mess hall. "I know that it's hard for you to watch everyone else playing sports while you can't. But losing your temper and taking it out on your friends isn't going to make you feel any better."

"But I do feel better," Jenna said.

"Are you sure about that?" Andie asked softly. "Listen, I think you could be a terrific coach for 4A, but one of the most important traits of a good coach is patience. The girls on your team may not play as well as you'd like them to, but they won't ever get better unless they learn how. They can learn from you."

"Did you see the way they played today?" Jenna sighed. "There's no hope."

"Just try to give them a shot, and see what happens," Andie said. "Please?"

"I'll try," she said, just to make Andie drop it.

"Thanks, sweetie," Andie said. "I knew I could count on you."

When Jenna sat down at the bunk table, though, she was met with silence. No one would look at her, let alone talk to her. Jenna sighed and scooped up a forkful of ravioli. Well, she'd eat her lunch, and then she'd figure out how to handle her friends. But before Jenna could take a bite of her food, Nat let out a scream.

"Hot! Hot! Hot!" she cried, grabbing for her glass of bug juice.

Suddenly, there were shouts from all over the mess hall, and Jenna saw Alex and Brynn suck down their glasses of bug juice in one gulp. Adam, Simon and Devon were all doing the same.

Pete came running out of the kitchen. "What's wrong?" he asked.

"I don't know," Andie said. "Is there something wrong with the food?"

Nat nodded her head violently and pointed to the ravioli before downing her entire glass.

Pete and Andie each took the tiniest taste of ravioli.

"Tabasco," Pete choked, "and lots of it."

"Oh, Jenna," Andie said, disappointment shining in her eyes. "I thought we agreed you wouldn't do this again."

"I didn't do anything!" Jenna cried in disbelief, putting down her fork.

"I'm afraid I'm having trouble believing you this time, Jenna," Dr. Steve said, walking over to her. "Last year you promised that you wouldn't pull any more pranks like this. But now our ravioli is spiked with Tabasco. And with all the pranks that have gone on in the last couple of days, the evidence is stacking up against you."

"But *none* of this was me!" Jenna cried.

Dr. Steve just frowned. "Please don't make me call

your parents again like I had to last year. I don't like punishing my campers, but I will if this continues."

"But I'm telling the truth," Jenna pleaded with Andie once Dr. Steve walked away.

"Look, Jenna," Andie said. "I know you're upset about your leg. But, please. You can't keep doing this."

Jenna's heart sank as she glanced around the table and saw all of her bunkmates glaring at her. It didn't matter what she said...no one was going to believe her.

"Can I be excused?" she said, her voice shaking. "I'm not hungry any more."

"Of course you're not," Chelsea snapped. "You probably already ate all of the good ravioli."

Jenna was too upset to even try to defend herself.

"All right," Andie said. "You can go back to the bunk. We'll meet you there before free swim."

Feeling tears starting at the corners of her eyes, Jenna tried to escape the mess hall before they started falling. She made it safely outside, but as she rounded the corner of the building, she spied Blake squatting behind the big rock by the lake, eating a bowl of ravioli, a huge grin on his face. Jenna stared in confusion. Wait a minute...he was scarfing down the ravioli, and he wasn't even breaking a sweat. That stuff had to be spicy enough to burn the hair off his head, so how could he stand to eat it? Unless...unless he had the only ravioli at camp that hadn't been spiked with Tabasco!

Jenna fumed as understanding dawned on her. So *Blake* was the one who'd been pulling these pranks all along.

A slow smile spread across Blake's face as he caught Jenna's eye. "I sure am glad I got some ravioli before you pulled your prank, Jenna," he said smoothly. "I hope you don't get into too much trouble for it." Then, before Jenna could say anything, Blake ditched his bowl in the trash can and walked into the mess hall, laughing.

Heat flashed through Jenna's cheeks as she slammed one of her crutches against the rock in frustration. This meant war. Blake had been setting her up all along, and now it was payback time. If everyone believed Jenna was pulling all these pranks, what was to keep her from actually doing them for real? She didn't have anything to lose, since they were blaming her anyway. And besides, she could find a way to frame Blake while she was at it, too. She'd teach him a lesson he'd never forget. She would come up with the prank to end all pranks, and she'd pull it during the final banquet at the end of this week. If she couldn't enjoy Colour War this year, she was going to make sure she *really* enjoyed the final banquet, uber-prank and all. It was time for the old Jenna to make a comeback in a very big way. She'd hatch a plan for the Best Prank Ever, and she'd start right now.

* * *

During the second banquet planning meeting that night, Jenna barely paid attention as Farrah and Kenny passed out craft supplies to make decorations for the Italian feast. Even though the whole theme had been her idea, she didn't really care about it any more. She had more important things to think about, like how to pull off the perfect prank to make the banquet dinner unforgettable. After camp was over, no one would remember the silly Italian flag candleholders they were making, or the rock-hard garlic bread, or the makeshift gondolas that *still* looked like canoes, no matter how hard the campers worked to disguise them. They wouldn't even remember Jenna's broken leg. But they would all remember a prank so magnificent, it would be forever ingrained in Camp Lakeview lore. All Jenna had to do was come up with it.

She finished painting one jelly jar with the Italian flag and moved on to her second, hoping she'd finish her assigned five soon so she could scope out the layout of the mess hall for prank ideas. Being on this planning committee had ended up giving her an advantage — she could investigate the ins and outs of the banquet plans and mess hall without anyone picking up on it. It was almost too good to be true. And because Sarah and Tiernan had given her the cold shoulder ever since she had walked into the room, Jenna didn't have any distractions. She finished her candleholders, dropped a tea light candle into each jar, and turned them in to Farrah.

"That was fast," Farrah said. "But there are five more jars where those came from. Want to do more?"

"Sure." Jenna smiled innocently. "But would you mind if I walked around for a few minutes first? My leg's getting kind of numb, and I think I need to stretch."

"No problem," Farrah said, concern in her eyes. "Just take it easy on that leg."

Jenna nodded, then slowly walked the perimeter of the mess hall. She couldn't let the animals from the nature shack loose in here again. That had been a mistake. No...she needed something funny and messy, but not *too* messy. She looked up to the ceiling, and her eyes lit on something that suddenly gave her a brilliant idea. She kept walking, making note of all the key spots she needed to make her prank work. And when she was finished, she knew, beyond a doubt, that this prank would be nothing short of sheer genius.

Afterwards, back in her bunk, she excused herself from a game of Monopoly to work out her idea. No one seemed the least bit bothered when she said she didn't want to play the game. Andie had the night off, and she'd looked so fab in her outfit and make-up when she'd left the bunk that everyone was convinced she had a date. Either way, Andie wasn't around to get Jenna involved in the bunk games. And thankfully, Mia didn't push the issue either, which relieved Jenna but also made her a little sad. She sighed. Of all the ways she'd pictured the summer ending, this definitely wasn't one of them. Now what did she have to look forward to? Getting into more trouble for things that weren't her fault, and finishing the summer without any of her friendships intact. Well, she had the prank to look forward to now, too. That was something good, at least.

Withdrawing to her bed, she propped her leg up on an extra pillow and got started. At the top of her stationery, she wrote the code name "Operation Drowned Rat". That's what she'd call it. The perfect name for the perfect prank. Next, she mapped out the prime target points in the mess hall that would set her plan into motion.

Once her notes and map of the mess hall were finished, she tucked them deep into the bottom of her backpack where they would be safe until the night of the banquet. Then she'd use them to execute her plan.

She'd pull off Operation Drowned Rat without a hitch. And with any luck, she'd be able to pin the blame on a certain blond-haired, blue-eyed boy she knew, too.

CHAPTER SEVEN

The next morning, Jenna woke up for the first time since she broke her leg with a glimmer in her eye.

"Good morning, ladies," she said. "Would anyone like an early-bird special on me?" She held up a handful of candy from her stash.

"No thanks, Jenna," Karen said timidly, seeming afraid that Jenna would start yelling at her.

"I'm not touching anything *you're* offering us," Chelsea said. "For all we know you could've filled your chocolates with ink or something."

Jenna just shrugged. "No biggie," she said. "We'll just save the candy for after sports."

A collective groan rose up from everyone at that, making Jenna laugh.

"Practice won't be that bad," she promised. "Things will go much better today. I feel really awful about the way I've been acting in sports lately, and I'm going to make it up to you, starting right now. You'll see." But as she glanced around at her friends, she was met with pair after pair of unsure eyes. And worse, now her friends actually looked a little afraid of her, too, as if they didn't know when she'd trick them all again.

"Well, I'm glad to see you're finally smiling again, Jenna," Andie told her proudly. "We all missed your cheerfulness. But I seriously hope this doesn't mean you've laced the boys' toilet seats with superglue or some other horrific thing."

"I already told you, I'm innocent," Jenna said, but this time she didn't let Andie's doubt get under her skin. Instead, she giggled and winked. "It's not a bad idea, though."

"Oh no," groaned Andie. "Please forget I said anything."

Jenna just smiled and whistled as she made her way into the bathroom with Alyssa for her shower. Things were looking up. Just thinking about Operation Drowned Rat was enough to put her in a good mood. Now all she had to do was figure out how to peg the blame on Blake afterwards. Once she did that, she'd be home free.

"Jenna," Alyssa said as she helped to wrap a garbage bag around Jenna's cast, "I really want to believe that you're telling the truth about all the pranks."

"You do?" Jenna said in surprise.

"Yup," Alyssa said. "I mean, it's the whole 'innocent until proven guilty' thing, right?" She shrugged. "But it's tough when we all saw the pranks you pulled off last summer. And all the other summers before that."

"I know." Jenna sighed, but then she smiled. "I just wish everyone else would believe I'm innocent, too."

She swung open the door to the shower stall, and suddenly a torrent of icy cold liquid splashed down on her head. Through the flood, she thought she heard Alyssa yell. But she herself was too stunned to say anything. She was still trying to catch her breath when she opened her eyes to see that her entire body was covered with slimy, green algae and stale pond water.

"What happened?" she gasped, shivering as she wiped some strands of algae off her face.

Alyssa picked up a bucket off the floor that was still dripping with water. "Someone rigged this to the top of the stall so it would tip over when you opened the door." She stood on tiptoe and peered up at the other shower stalls. "There are buckets rigged to every stall!"

Suddenly footsteps rang in the bunk, and Andie, Mia and the girls all appeared in the bathroom doorway.

"What happened?" Nat asked, gaping.

"At least your cast didn't get wet," Karen said optimistically. "It's really not that bad."

"Yes, it is," Jenna said.

"If you wanted a seaweed mask, Jenna," said Tori with a grin, "you could've just asked me for one."

"Okay, girls," Alyssa said matter-of-factly as she scooped up a tadpole and put it back in some water. "*Now* do you believe that Jenna's innocent?"

Through a slime haze, Jenna saw everyone nod.

"Well, since you couldn't go into the lake," Perry said, "I guess someone brought the lake to you instead."

"I could've survived without it, I think," Jenna muttered, staring at herself in the bathroom mirror.

Alyssa laughed. "You're not allowed to get depressed about this. It's way too funny for that. And besides, you just proved your innocence."

"Yeah, I guess that's a good thing," Jenna said, shaking goopy droplets from her hair. "And I think I know who the real prankster is."

"Who?" Andie asked.

"I'll tell you," Jenna said, then giggled. "But first, can someone please help me get this stuff out of my hair?"

Three shampoos and a dose of Nat's Aveda thermal conditioning rinse later, and Jenna had almost erased the memory of her tadpole hairdo. And thanks to Blake's little good-morning gift, everyone in the bunk finally believed that Jenna was innocent. During breakfast she quietly explained how she found him yesterday afternoon, sneaking Tabasco-free raviolis.

"But there's one thing I still don't get. What about the snake in Blake's pillowcase?" Alyssa asked. "The first prank was played on *him*."

Jenna nodded between bites of soggy scrambled eggs. "An act of self-sabotage. It's part of the fine art of pranking. I did it myself when I first started pranking, too."

"So how do we know it wasn't you who set up the buckets in the shower, then?" Chelsea asked. "You could've been trying to fool us."

"Come on, Chelsea," Alyssa said. "Jenna couldn't have set up all those buckets by herself...on crutches. This prank has Blake Wetherly written all over it."

"Well," Tori huffed. "I think somebody should put purple food colouring in *his* toothpaste for a change."

Jenna smiled. Oh, if they only knew what she had planned for him. But that was her little secret, and she wanted to keep it that way.

"Who does he think he is, anyway?" Chelsea fumed. "Just because his parents are filthy rich doesn't mean he can get away with being a juvenile delinquent."

"The problem is that we don't have any concrete evidence," Andie said. "I talked to Kenny while you guys were helping Jenna get cleaned up, because I wanted to see if he'd noticed Blake, or any of the other boys, missing from the bunk at all. He says Blake didn't move once all night."

"The other guys don't know anything, either," Mia said. "If they did, they would have definitely turned him in for the ravioli trick."

"No kidding," Jenna said. "There's no way they'd let someone mess with their food and get away with it."

"But Blake does whatever he wants, whenever he wants. Everybody knows he doesn't follow the rules. Half the time he doesn't even participate in the activities, and nobody ever notices. It's because he's Dr. Steve's nephew," Alyssa said. "Everyone knows better than to mess with the camp director's family."

"Well, we'll just have to keep an eye out, then," Andie said. She turned to Jenna. "I'm sorry I didn't believe you before."

"But you can't blame us for thinking it was you," Chelsea said. "After the way you completely ruined the square dance last year, what were we supposed to think? You were the queen of pranks."

And I still am, Jenna thought, *and I'll prove it in just a few more days.* But then her conscience kicked into gear to remind her how good it felt to finally be trusted again. Her friends were back on her side. Did she really want to mess that up with Operation Drowned Rat? She could just forget about the whole thing. But where was the fun in that? If she didn't follow through with her plan, Blake would get off scot-free. Nuh-uh. Operation Drowned Rat was still on, no matter what. But for now, she could at least make sure her friendships were back on track until the time came for the queen of pranks to reappear.

"I don't blame you for not believing in me," she said. "Especially with the way I've been acting lately. I'm sorry about losing my temper yesterday on the soccer field. I shouldn't have been so critical. You guys are doing a great job playing. And no matter what teams you're on for Colour War, I'm sure you're all going to be terrific." She sighed. "I was just wishing that I could be out there with you, you know?"

"We understand," Tori told her. "I wish you could be out there with us, too. I'm way better at makeovers than sports. We need help."

"We know you'll make the best Colour War cheerleader a bunk could ask for," Mia said.

Jenna tried not to visibly cringe at the word "cheerleader", because it still reminded her all over again that, no matter what her friends tried to do to make her feel better, she'd still be left out for most of Colour War. The competitions started in two days, and she couldn't bear the thought of sitting out the whole war. And now that her friends believed she was innocent, they'd never blame her for Operation Drowned Rat. Instead, Blake would seem like the most obvious culprit. She pushed away her feelings of guilt about betraying her friends. They wanted to get back at Blake, too, so they'd understand Operation Drowned Rat, wouldn't they? Her victory would be at the final banquet instead of Colour War, but it would be just as sweet.

Fixing things with her bunk was one thing, but fixing things with Alex proved to be a lot more complicated than Jenna expected. As she sat down in ceramics and pulled out her moulding clay, she replayed everything that had happened after breakfast. In sports, things had gone a lot more smoothly on the basketball court than they had on the soccer field for the last week. Jenna had taken a deep breath and relaxed, enjoying watching her friends play for the first time since she'd broken her leg. When she gave Nat, Alyssa and Karen pointers about shooting hoops or passing, she didn't yell or criticize. Instead, she just calmly made suggestions and then sat back and watched them play.

But dealing with Alex was tougher. Alex was

avoiding her at all costs, and even when Jenna congratulated her on a good game after Alex shot the nothing-but-net final winning point, Alex just pretended that she hadn't heard. Later, during free swim, Jenna tried to catch Alex's eye from where she was sitting on the beach, but Alex just stuck to the water, completely ignoring her. Now, as Jenna tried to bend and tweak her clay into something resembling a vase, she wished she were more talented at ceramics *and* at apologizing to Alex. Clearly, she needed more practice at both to get it right.

"The only flowers that would look good in that thing," Blake said, sliding his stool over to inspect her work, "are dead ones."

"At least I'm trying," Jenna said. "You haven't made a single thing so far." She glared at him. "But you must be too busy rigging buckets to shower heads to bother with legitimate camp activities, right?"

"So what if I am?" he asked. "You can't prove anything. I just wish I'd been there to see it come down." He laughed. "But the Tabasco trick...now *that* I saw. The look on Uncle Steve's face when he took that huge mouthful of ravioli at lunch?" He laughed. "Classic, just classic."

Jenna giggled in spite of herself. "It was impressive for your first big prank." Then she glared at him. "But don't let that go to your head. If I'd done it, I would've put it in the bug juice, too. I would've had kids diving into the lake for a drink."

Blake thought about that, then nodded. "That *would've* been awesome," he said with a touch of respect.

Jenna laughed. So, maybe she and Blake had one thing in common – a sense of humour. Maybe he wasn't a total lost cause after all. Maybe, behind Blake's attitude, there was a nicer, more genuine person that Jenna might enjoy being friends with (even if he *was* a boy).

"You're just lucky it wasn't Andie who got in the shower first today," Jenna said. "She would've turned you in to Dr. Steve for sure."

Blake snorted. "I'd like to see her try it," he said. "Nobody's ever done that to me. Not with my family. Besides, Uncle Steve would never believe her. He loves me."

"Why?" Jenna said. "Because you fake being good around him? If he knew what you were really doing, I'm pretty sure he wouldn't think you were so perfect any more."

"He doesn't know," Blake said, "and he never will."

As soon as Blake pulled his little-rich-boy routine, anger bubbled up inside Jenna. She couldn't believe him! For a minute there, she'd actually been enjoying talking to him. But now he was just back to being a real snot.

"You know," Jenna said, "if you'd get off your high horse, you'd see you're just like everybody else here. Except more stuck-up, and not as nice."

Blake blinked in surprise, opened his mouth as though he wanted to say something, and then closed it again. For once, he didn't have much to say. He was quiet for the rest of the class and left without saying another word.

Jenna carried her finished vase back to her bunk with a smile. Sure, her vase was still droopy and lopsided. But she was satisfied that maybe she'd finally given Blake something to think about. On the other hand, maybe he was just plotting a way to dump all of her belongings into the lake tonight. There was nothing scarier than a prankster out for revenge. She knew that better than anyone. She'd just have to keep a close lookout tonight. And in the meantime, maybe there was another way to teach him a lesson first.

After the lights went out in the bunk that night, Jenna waited until everyone had grown still, breathing deeply. Andie was the on-duty counsellor tonight, so she'd be gone for the next couple of hours. And since Mia slept deeper than a hibernating bear, there wasn't much chance of her waking up. The coast was clear. Jenna slipped out of bed as quietly as she could and put on the shorts and T-shirt she'd hidden under her pillow earlier. There was no way she could sleep right now, especially when all she'd been doing for the last half-hour was rehashing all the awful things she'd said to Alex yesterday, wishing she could take them all back. Alex had blown her off all day today, so Jenna figured her only chance was to catch her off guard so that she wouldn't be able to ignore her any more. Now was her chance. If the two of them could laugh with each other again, then Jenna would know that everything was okay between them. And Jenna knew just how to get Alex to laugh tonight.

She grabbed the photo Adam had taken of Alex and slid it into the front pouch of her pullover. Then she propped herself up on her crutches and stealthily made her way to Natalie's bed.

"Nat," she whispered, giving her a gentle nudge. "Wake up."

"Huh?" Nat said groggily. "What's the matter? Do you need help getting to the bathroom?"

Jenna grinned in the dark. "Nope. I need to borrow your make-up bag. Just for a little while. I'll bring it back in perfect shape. I promise."

Nat sat up, eyeing Jenna suspiciously. "What are you up to, you little sneak?" she whispered.

"Let's just say, there's a certain boy in a certain bunk tonight who's not going to recognize himself when he looks in the mirror tomorrow morning."

"Okay," Nat finally agreed, giggling quietly. "But if anyone asks, you took my make-up bag without permission. I'd prefer to be an anonymous accomplice."

"Got it," Jenna said. "Thanks." She slid the make-up bag into the pocket of her pullover and took a few steps to the door. She froze when her crutches squeaked loudly on the floor, but no one budged, except Nat, who just buried her head in her pillow to stifle a giggle.

Once Jenna was safely outside, she sighed with relief. So far, so good. But before she headed to the boys' bunks, she needed to make one important stop. She had to talk to Alex, and she had to talk to her now.

It was tough to manoeuvre in the dark on crutches without being noisy, especially with the make-up bag in her front pocket throwing her a little off balance. She stumbled a few times but caught herself. And lucky for her, tonight the crickets and cicadas were out in full force, filling the night air with deafening singing that drowned out the crunch of her crutches in the dirt. With a full moon to help light her path, Jenna finally managed to find her way to the 4C bunk, and then inside to Alex's bed.

Jenna was just about to wake her up when Alex's eyes popped open. She took one look at Jenna and pulled her pillow over her head. "If you're coming to murder me in my sleep, I'm sure there's a camp rule about that sort of thing," she mumbled through the pillow.

Jenna lifted one corner of the pillow and smiled at Alex. "I come in peace," she said in her best imitation of an alien, and Alex, much to Jenna's relief, broke into a quiet laugh.

"Can we talk outside?" Jenna asked.

"No more wicked-witch routine?" Alex asked tentatively.

"Not unless you steal the Swedish Fish out of my candy stash." Jenna giggled. "Come on. I need your help."

When they were safely outside and heading towards the boys' bunk, Alex turned to Jenna. "Okay, spill it. And this better be good."

Jenna took a deep breath. "First, I wanted to say I'm sorry for how I acted the past couple of days," she said. "I know I've been a real jerk to you lately."

"True," Alex said, "but I owe you an apology, too. I'm

sorry I didn't believe you weren't pulling the pranks."

"So you know it was Blake?" Jenna asked.

Alex nodded. "Tori filled me in during free swim today. I'm sorry I didn't trust you."

"Thanks," Jenna said. "But I don't blame you for losing your patience with me when I was acting so bratty. I guess I'm just a little jealous that you're getting to play all my favourite sports and I'm not. And on top of that, I'm going to have to watch you kick butt in Colour War, too." Jenna sighed. "I'm missing the whole thing."

"Not the whole thing," Alex said. "Did you talk to Andie? Why can't you be in the Scrabble tournament or something?"

"Are you kidding?" Jenna said. "You and Chelsea are the Scrabble queens. The only thing I've ever been really good at is sports."

"You might be good at other things, too, if you give it a try," Alex said. "I can't always do the things I want to do, either, because of my diabetes."

"You can still play soccer," Jenna said.

"Yeah." Alex nodded. "But I'd kill for a chocolate bar right now. And you can have one of those, and I can't."

Jenna sighed. "True. I don't think I could survive without candy the way you do. But that still doesn't fix my Colour War problem. The rally is tomorrow night, and after that, I'll be benching it until the banquet."

"We'll figure something out," Alex said. "Besides, you'll be back next year, kicking my tail all over the soccer field and basketball court again. Your leg will be back to one hundred per cent. And who knows? Maybe it will be a super-strong bionic leg after you get your cast off."

"I can only hope," Jenna said, laughing. "Thanks for putting up with my attitude."

"No problem," Alex said. "You'd do the same for me if I couldn't play. Just make sure the attitude doesn't make a sudden comeback. Deal?"

"Deal," Jenna said, giving Alex a hug. "Oh, and I have something for you, too." She pulled the photo from her pocket. "Adam asked me to give this to you a few days ago. I know I should've given it to you earlier, but with things all weird between us, I didn't want to. And I'm so sorry for that."

Jenna waited for Alex to yell at her, which she knew she deserved. But instead, Alex took the photo and slowly held it up so she could see it in the moonlight. Then a huge smile spread across her face. "Did he really take this?" she whispered excitedly, her eyes lighting up. "What did he say when he gave it to you?"

Jenna groaned. "I take it back. I should've kept the photo." But when Alex slugged her on the arm, she smiled. "If you ask me, I think he likes you. I mean, come on, he sure has been talking about you a lot lately." She shuddered at the thought. "And that's a pretty strong hint, if you ask me. But playing matchmaker for you guys has been creeping me out, so here's the deal. From now on, you and Adam talk to each other, instead of to me. Do you think you can handle that?"

Alex nodded enthusiastically. "I can't believe he printed this for me," she said dreamily.

"Earth to Alex," Jenna said. "Can we continue on our mission now?"

"All right." Alex reluctantly tucked the photo into her jacket as they reached Adam's bunk. "But aren't you going to tell me what we're doing here?"

"Preppy boy Blake is going to get an extreme makeover tonight," Jenna said, pulling the make-up bag out of her pocket. "Do you think purple or pink eyeshadow goes better with his complexion?"

"Let's try both and find out," Alex said, and they both giggled.

Blake was one sound sleeper. He didn't move once, even when Jenna dabbed some blue glitter mascara on his eyelashes. Of course, the fact that Kenny's snoring was louder than a freight train made their task a lot easier to accomplish. Jenna was sure that none of the boys could hear their footsteps over Kenny's snore symphony.

"Perfect," Alex whispered as Jenna put the finishing touches on Blake with some Pomegranate Passion lipstick. "He's a masterpiece."

"He sure is," a voice said behind them, and Jenna and Alex both nearly jumped out of their skin. There was Adam in his pyjamas, grinning at them.

"Oh my gosh," Alex said. "Adam, you're not going to tell, are you?"

"No way," Adam said. "I'm going to set my alarm so I'll be the first one up to take a picture of the newest Lakeview cover girl. The photos will be perfect for the camp newsletter." He bent down to inspect Jenna's handiwork. "He could use a little more blush, though, don't you think?"

Jenna dabbed on a little more while Blake slept on, and then she and Alex turned to go.

"You go first," Alex whispered. "I'll be right there."

Jenna waited just outside, and a minute later Alex scooted out the door, beaming.

"If this involves kissing," Jenna said, "I don't want to hear it. I'll never be able to look at my brother without gagging again."

"Of course not," Alex said. Her eyes glowed happily. "I just wanted to tell him thank you for the photo. And he asked if he could call me after camp is over."

"Too much information," Jenna said, making sure she sounded as melodramatic as possible. "Come on, et's get out of here before someone other than Adam wakes up."

Jenna smiled as she and Alex walked back to their bunks. She was happy that everything was okay with Alex again, and she was even happier about the prank she just pulled. There were times in life when revenge was oh-so-sweet.

CHAPTER EIGHT

Even with her crutches, Jenna still beat the rest of her bunk to breakfast the next morning. The other girls weren't too far behind her, though, because with everyone in camp preparing for the Colour War kick-off that night, the adrenaline was pumping. Jenna was getting excited, too. Not about Colour War, but about what she'd accomplish after Colour War with Operation Drowned Rat. And this morning she had another reason to be excited, too. She wasn't even surprised when Alex met her at the mess-hall doors.

"You couldn't wait, either?" Jenna asked, grinning.

"No way," Alex said. "I'm dying to see if some of our makeover survived the night."

They walked through the doors together, and sure enough, there was Blake, his head bent low – a bit too low – over his bowl of oatmeal.

Jenna struggled to hold in her laughter as they

walked over to his table. She could still see smudges of mascara around his eyes, and his lips did have a pinkish glow to them. Poor guy. Too bad she had used long-wearing make-up.

"Hey, Blake," Jenna said sweetly, with the most innocent smile she could muster. "How'd your enjoy your beauty sleep last night?"

Jenna wasn't sure what to expect – a temper tantrum or the cold shoulder. But amazingly, Blake broke into a good-natured laugh instead. "So *you* were the ones who glamorized me last night. I knew it!"

"You're not mad?" Alex asked.

"Hey, all's fair in pranks and war, right?" he said. "Besides, my skin feels so soft and clean," he caressed his cheek, doing his best impression of a model in a make-up ad. "Just like a baby's."

Jenna grinned. "That purple was the perfect shade for your eyes."

"I agree." He batted his eyelashes. "But did you have to use waterproof mascara?"

"It's the only way to go." Jenna nodded as she walked away with Alex. "It comes out way better in photos."

"Photos?" Blake called after her. "What photos?"

* * *

131

When Jenna walked onto the basketball court, the last thing she expected was the brightly wrapped box that Nat handed to her with a huge grin.

"For you," she said, "from all of us."

Alyssa, Karen, Perry, Tori and all the other girls from the bunk gathered around Jenna with expectant faces.

"It's to say thank you," Andie explained, "for being such a good sport about, well, not playing sports."

Jenna opened the box and pulled out an adorable baby tee that said LAKEVIEW'S #1 COACH, JENNA BLOOM on the front and GET YOUR BLOOM ON! on the back.

"Nat made it in her arts and crafts class," Mia explained.

"I love it," she said quietly, feeling tears well up in her eyes. She looked at her friends. "But I don't deserve it. I've been anything but a good sport *or* a good coach. I lost my temper..."

"True," Chelsea said.

"...and yelled at all of you..."

"Yup," Perry confirmed.

"...and threw a major pity party for myself on a daily basis!" Jenna cried.

"All of the above," Alyssa said. "But we still love you."

"Which is why we came up with a plan," Jessie added in.

Andie put her arm around Jenna. "Actually, it was Alex who came to me with the idea after breakfast this morning, and then we all went to talk to Dr. Steve about it."

"What?" Jenna asked.

"Well," Mia said, "we know how much you're going to miss playing sports in Colour War this year, but we're going to replace blob tag with a different event. One I think you'll really enjoy competing in."

"And your sweet tooth will thank us," Chelsea said. Jenna couldn't believe that Chelsea had been involved in this, too. It wasn't like her to stick her neck out for anybody. But there was a first for everything.

"It's a pie-eating contest," Andie said. "A group event, and we'd like you to represent us in it."

"Seriously?" Jenna said, getting excited. "All-you-can-eat pie, huh?" A smile broke across her face. "That's my kind of contest. So, what sort of pie will it be?"

"Dr. Steve's keeping that a secret from all of us," Andie said. "But if it has sugar in it, I bet you'll like it."

"I know I will." Then she smiled. "Thanks so much for doing that for me. You guys are the best." She held out her crutches. "Group hug!"

Everyone piled in, careful not to tip her over, since she was stuck right in the middle.

"Okay," she finally said as she noticed the girls from

4C showing up for the game. "Enough mush. It's time to get your Bloom on!"

The girls clapped and cheered and ran onto the court, and it was right then that Jenna got her idea. Her friends had all been so sweet to her, and now she wanted to thank them, and she knew just how to do it. Once the girls were all dribbling balls and passing them back and forth to warm up, Jenna turned to Andie.

"Andie," she said, "would you mind if I went to the ceramics workshop for a little while? Maybe Chelsea can take over coaching, just for today. There's a project I need to work on that I want to finish before the Colour War rally tonight. It's really important."

"Sure, Jenna," Andie said. "But the girls will miss your coaching."

"I have a sneaking suspicion that Chelsea will be a great coach." Jenna winked at Andie. "And next to her, I bet I'll seem like a piece of cake."

"So true." Andie laughed. "Just meet us back at the mess hall for lunch, okay?"

Jenna nodded, but she was already walking away. She couldn't wait to get to ceramics and start working. As she walked, she thought about how patient and understanding everyone had been with her ever since she'd broken her leg. And now she even had something to look forward to in Colour War. A pie-eating contest was way more fun than Scrabble, that was for sure, and she might even stand a chance of winning, too. She was back in action, thanks to her friends. For the first time in almost two weeks, she wasn't dreading Colour War. She was looking forward to it. And then there'd be the great banquet afterwards with the music and awards and – yikes! Jenna froze mid-step. The banquet was when Operation Drowned Rat would come down. But now that everything was going so great, how could she pull the prank and risk ruining it all again? Even if she managed to successfully frame Blake for Operation Drowned Rat, the banquet would still be a wash, thanks to her. If her friends found out, they'd never forgive her...not this time. And they mattered more than anything. She couldn't do it...not even getting back at Blake seemed so important now, not with her friends by her side. And the perfect prank didn't seem so perfect any more, either.

She stopped at one of the outdoor trash cans and pulled her notes for Operation Drowned Rat out of her backpack. She stared at them for a minute, then threw them into the trash can. She didn't want to carry through with her prank after all, not when she was going to have an honest-to-goodness part in Colour War. The banquet would be amazing without the prank, as long as she had her friends to share it with.

*   *   *

She worked for the next hour on her ceramics project, and again that afternoon in ceramics class. She left lunch as soon as she was finished eating to get back to work. Now, as she pulled her tray of beads out of the kiln and began to string them together, she smiled at her progress. She'd have just enough time to finish these before the start of Colour War, and they'd be perfect.

When Blake showed up to class, ten minutes late as usual, even he surveyed her handiwork with a glimmer of admiration.

"Not bad," he said. "Your coffee mugs and vases were pretty pathetic, but those actually look half-decent."

Jenna rolled her eyes but laughed. "Coming from you, that almost sounded like a compliment."

"It was an accident." Blake grinned. "It won't happen again." He pulled his own project from the craft shelf and set it on the table, and for the first time Jenna really looked at it.

"Wow," she said. "That's...beautiful." It was a small sculpture of a horse galloping, so carefully detailed that Jenna could even see the hairs in its mane. "You're a real artist. But I never saw you working on it."

"I don't like doing artwork in front of other people, so I worked a lot during free time instead."

Jenna blinked in surprise. This was a whole new side of Blake she'd never seen before. "I thought you hated ceramics," she said.

"Nah," Blake said. "I take sculpting classes at home, but, you know, it's *my* thing. I just didn't want to answer a million questions about it when I came here."

"That makes sense," Jenna said. "I feel that way about my parents' divorce when I'm at home. But how did you learn to sculpt horses like that?"

Blake shrugged. "Practice, I guess. He's my horse back home. His name's War Bonnet." He looked down at the horse and smiled. "When I'm at home, I ride him every day."

"You must miss him," Jenna said.

"Sure," Blake said casually, but Jenna could tell that he did. He cleared his throat and squirmed in his seat. "So, Uncle Steve told me about the pie-eating contest," he said. "I guess that beats Scrabble any day."

"You know it," she said. "Sugar can never take the place of soccer, but it comes in a close second."

"I hate pie." He grimaced. "But sports...I could handle that."

"Does that mean you're actually thinking about participating in Colour War?" Jenna asked.

"Uncle Steve's going to make me, no matter what, so I have to stick with my team, right?"

"Yeah." She nodded. "It's just surprising, that's all. I mean, the last couple of days you've been more interested in pulling pranks than participating in the rest of the camp activities. And you've never been nice to me before, until today. So what's with the big switch?"

Blake thought about that for a minute before answering. "Sometimes I get treated differently because of the kind of life I have," he said. "Kids just want to hear me talk all about my dad's jet, or our house in Lake Como. You're the first person I've met in a while who wasn't afraid to be honest with me. Like you were yesterday."

"So," Jenna said, "maybe camp isn't such a huge waste of your time after all?"

"Maybe," he said.

"You'll love Colour War," Jenna said. "And the final banquet is awesome."

"Yeah, I'm looking forward to that," Blake said. Then, to Jenna's surprise, he gave an honest-to-goodness, genuine smile.

The rest of the day flew by in a flurry of excitement, and by dinner time the counsellors could hardly keep order in the mess hall. A few food fights broke out, but Kenny, Andie and the CITs put a stop to them before anything got really out of control. Jenna loved every second of it, though. This was what always happened just before the start of Colour War, when everyone was so pumped up that sitting still became completely impossible. As soon as the sun set, everyone met at the campfire for the rally. It was so muggy out that it seemed almost ridiculous even to have a campfire, but there was no way they were going to break that tradition.

"Wow," Jenna said as she sat down with her bunkmates around the crackling fire. She'd been coming to camp for so many years that she thought she'd seen just about everything, but even she was impressed when she saw how the counsellors and CITs had decorated the campfire area.

A huge Colour War banner painted in red and blue letters was strung up between two of the bigger pine trees, and streamers and balloon clusters hung from every tree branch Jenna could see. All the counsellors and CITs were wearing red and blue wigs and face paint, and even Dr. Steve was wearing a huge, puffy, red-and-blue-striped wig.

He lifted his megaphone to his face and yelled out the start of the Lakeview camp cheer, "We're Camp Lakeview!"

"We're Camp Lakeview!" sang out all the campers.

"We're gonna tell the world..." he shouted.

"Who we are!" answered the campers. They all stood up and stomped their feet, until the entire campground sounded like a herd of stampeding elephants. "Lakeview campers rule, yes we do! Lakeview, Lakeview, we love you!"

Dr. Steve passed the megaphone to Kenny, who shouted out, "Let's hear it from bunk 4E." Adam's bunkmates huddled together and yelled their bunk cheer as loud as they could.

"That was loud," Dr. Steve said, looking at the noise-o-meter he had in his hand. It was a special gauge for measuring noise levels that Dr. Steve had bought from a hardware store earlier in the summer.

4C gave their cheer next, and Jenna laughed as she watched Alex, Sarah and Brynn's faces turn red as they screamed as loud as they could.

"Louder," Dr. Steve said. "But still not loud enough."

Then Andie took the megaphone and turned to 4A. Jenna hooked her arms through the other girls' until their whole bunk formed a tight half circle. "Let's hear it!" Andie shouted.

Jenna threw her head back and yelled at the top of her lungs with her bunkmates:

"The bunk 4A chicks can't be beat!
We're smart and strong and super-sweet.
Watch out or we'll take you down.
We'll kick your butts right out of town!"

They erupted into a deafening round of applause, foot-stomping, and war whoops as Dr. Steve watched his noise-o-meter.

"Definitely ear-splitting!" he shouted. "Silly String 'em!"

Jenna high-fived her friends as the other campers doused them in Silly String. All the counsellors had passed out cans of Silly String to the campers before the rally, and so far, every bunk had done something to get themselves doused. It was all part of the fun.

Jenna laughed so hard that her stomach ached as she pulled Silly String out of her hair and off her clothes and piled it on Andie and Mia instead. All the campers were making sure that the counsellors and CITs were covered from head to toe in string, too. Jenna sang camp songs and yelled cheers until her throat hurt, smiling the entire time. She loved how everyone in camp was coming together tonight – the younger kids and the older ones. Everyone was a team, united in their love for Lakeview. It was this friendship and fun that made her keep coming back to camp, year after year. It was the best feeling in the world.

Once the Lakeview camp song had been sung, the campers all looked at Dr. Steve, waiting to see if he'd give any hint about the Colour War team assignments, which they wouldn't get until the morning. But he wasn't about to give anything away.

"Okay," Dr. Steve smiled. "Let's keep tonight prank free so you'll all be well rested for tomorrow's games. You'll get your team assignments when you wake up tomorrow morning."

"Look at him," Jenna grumbled. "He's so proud of the fact that he has a secret no one else knows." She was especially impatient to get the assignments, because she couldn't wait to hand out her special surprise to everyone first thing tomorrow morning.

Suddenly, flashes of bright light filled the night sky. Jenna looked up as red and blue fireworks exploded over the lake, sending twinkling sparks that rained down on the water. She smiled. Even with her broken leg, she had a happy feeling that this was going to be one of the best Colour Wars ever.

CHAPTER NINE

Jenna's eyes shot open even before the sun peeked through the window of the bunk.

"Rise and shine, sleepyheads!" she sang to her bunkmates. "Don't you want to know your team assignments?"

"I'd rather sleep, thank you," Alyssa said, pulling her sheets over her head.

"You are so warped, Jenna," Chelsea quipped. "It's not even light out yet."

"Wake up! Wake up!" Jenna sing-songed, rapping on Nat's and Perry's beds with her crutches. Then she flipped on the bunk lights just as a barrage of pillows showered her from all corners of the room.

Tori sat straight up in bed. "I can't believe you woke me up before the alarm went off." She pointed to her face, which was completely covered in blue goop. "This rehydrating mask needs at least six hours for full moisturizing potential."

"Oh, get over it! It's the start of Colour War!" Jenna cried jubilantly, throwing up her hands. "Hey..." She took a closer look at Tori. "What's wrong with your forehead?"

"What?" Tori gasped, her hands flying up to her hairline. "Oh please, please, please tell me I didn't get a zit."

"You've got a big red dot right in the middle of all that blue," Jenna said. "It looks like...paint."

Her eyes flickered around the room. "We all have dots painted on our foreheads! Either red or blue." She squealed. "Our team assignments!" She whipped around to see Andie and Mia giggling from their beds. "You sneaks!"

"We did it while you were sleeping last night," Mia said, stifling a yawn.

Jenna went around the room, taking a tally. Once she finished, she had the breakdown. Nat, Alyssa, Chelsea, Tori and Perry were on the Red team. Anna, Lauren, Jessie and Karen were on the Blue. Then she froze. "But what colour am I?" she cried. "Somebody help me."

"Red!" Nat said, jumping out of bed to hug her.

"Red!" Jenna repeated, her smile spreading. "The colour of victory!"

*　　*　　*

144

Maybe she'd spoken too soon. The Blues stood more than a chance. From the looks of things at the kick-off breakfast, the Blues actually had the upper hand. As Jenna made a mental list of who was on what team from the other bunks, her spirits sank. Grace, Abby, Priya and Candace were all Reds, which was great. But Alex, Brynn, Sarah, Valerie, Tiernan and Gaby were Blues, which was trouble. As soon as breakfast was over and everyone left the mess hall to head to the first event of the day, Alex and Sarah stopped on the lawn and yelled out a cheer with the rest of the Blues. Jenna tried to organize the Reds to give a counter-cheer, but she wasn't quick enough, and the chance slipped by.

"We'll get 'em next time," Jenna said, struggling to make her voice sound optimistic.

But then Chelsea said what Jenna'd really been thinking but was afraid to say.

"We're going to get killed in sports," Chelsea whined. "Alex and Sarah will be impossible to beat." She glared at Jenna. "What did you have to go and break your leg for, anyway? Talk about stupid. How are we supposed to win the soccer tournament tomorrow with two prima donnas and a drama queen on our team?"

"Thanks for the vote of confidence, Chelsea," Tori piped up. "But I'll have you know that Nat and I painted our nails with Nails of Steel strengthening polish last night so we wouldn't worry about breaking them. We're ready to do battle."

Nat nodded. "And Simon's a Red, too," she added proudly. "He's really good at sports, so I bet he'll bring home some wins for the guys, too."

"We can take on the Blues, no problem," Grace, one of the Reds from 4C, chimed in enthusiastically, her curls bouncing wildly. "I've been rehearsing my dribble for the last three days. A good actress can play all sorts of parts, including a soccer pro."

"The Blues aren't going to know what hit 'em," Jenna said encouragingly, doing her best to hide her doubts. She turned to Nat, Tori, Chelsea, Alyssa and Perry. "I know we haven't played that well up till now."

"That's an understatement," Alyssa said.

"But we can," Jenna said. "Lots of underdogs overcome the odds. We just have to do our best." She banged her crutch on the mess-hall railing. "Can I have the attention of everyone in 4A and 4C, please?"

The girls from both bunks stopped outside the mess hall and turned towards her. Jenna slid her backpack from her shoulder and pulled out the surprise she'd wanted to give everyone last night but hadn't been able to until she knew the team assignments.

"I made these for everyone in both of our bunks." She held up ten red and ten blue necklaces, each made with the ceramic beads she'd worked so hard on yesterday. Each red bead had just the tiniest flecks of blue in it, and each blue bead held a little red. "It turns out, jewellery was the only thing I made in ceramics that didn't fall apart," she joked, making everyone giggle.

"I knew you'd be great at jewellery!" Nat said.

"They're friendship beads," Jenna said, passing them out by colour to the two bunks, "to remind us that before we are frenemies, we are friends, first and for ever."

"What a great idea, sweetie," Andie said, hugging Jenna. "And you're right. Our friendships are what count more than anything, and no matter what, now everyone has a reminder of that. I'm so proud of you for remembering what's most important!"

"Most important," Jenna agreed. "But we Reds are still going to make the Blues eat our dust!"

If fun included getting massacred in the first division event, then the Reds were definitely having a lot of it. The basketball tournament wasn't so much a competition as it was a catastrophe.

"Jenna," Andie said from the sidelines, "you're pacing so much, you're digging a hole in the ground."

Jenna looked away from the basketball court for the first time since the game had started and saw that she was actually creating a small dirt trail where her crutches had been clumping across the grass. "I can't help it. It's the only thing I can use this stupid thing for." She gave her cast a frustrated thump with her crutch, feeling totally helpless watching from the sidelines.

She sighed, refocused her attention on the court, and clapped her hands encouragingly. "Come on, Reds!" she shouted. "You can do it!" Her eyes flickered briefly to the scoreboard, and it was all she could do not to throw in her crutches then and there. Fourth quarter and the score was 20 to...2?!

As much as Jenna hated to admit it, she knew Chelsea had had a valid point at breakfast. The Reds had only managed to score two measly points so far, and that was only because the referee had granted the Reds two free shots after the Blues got penalties for holding. Miracle of miracles, Nat and Tori had each made a shot. But it seemed that they could only actually make it into the basket when they were shooting while standing completely still. Making a shot on the court while the game was in motion? Forget about it.

The sad truth was that the game had been one disaster after another. It all started when Chelsea tried to pass the basketball to Tori in the first quarter and Tori screamed and fumbled so badly that she dropped the ball straight into the hands of the Blues. Then, things went from bad to worse when Grace and Nat collided trying to catch the ball in the second quarter. By the third, it was obvious that this tournament was turning into Humiliation 101 for the Reds. Now, in the fourth, Jenna was just hoping her teammates would live to see the end of the game.

With one minute left on the clock, Jenna called a time out and motioned her dreary-looking team into a huddle.

"You guys are doing great," she said. "We still have time to make a comeback."

"Are you kidding?" Chelsea cried. "Please tell me what grand plan you have for making up eighteen points in one minute."

"I'm not talking about winning," Jenna said. "Who cares about that? We're here to have fun. Right?"

Silence.

"Right?" she asked again louder.

"Right," Alyssa, Tori and Nat answered weakly.

"So," Jenna said, happy that she'd gotten at least a lukewarm response from her teammates, "you may not win, but you can still play like a team. Right?"

"Right!" everyone shouted.

"Here's what we do," Jenna said, leaning over to whisper her plan.

Once everyone was back on the court, the clock started again and Jenna watched, holding her breath, as Alyssa started dribbling the ball down the court towards the Blues' basket. Then, in the manoeuvre Jenna had laid out beforehand, Alyssa faked a pass to Nat, who screamed perfectly on cue, sending Alex and Sarah both racing over to her to try to intercept the ball. That left Alyssa free to pass the ball to Tori, whose extra-strength nail polish apparently worked as she caught the ball, spun around, and handed it off to Grace.

"Yes!" Jenna yelled. "Go, Grace, go!"

Grace scooted past Gaby and Brynn, but when Alex and Sarah both closed in on her, panic hit her face.

"Now!" Jenna cried, and Grace focused on the basket, crouched down, and shot the ball into the air. Up, up, up – over everyone's heads...and straight into the basket just as the final buzzer sounded.

"Woo-hoo!" Jenna hollered, rushing onto the court as fast as her crutches could carry her. She gave Grace a bear hug while the rest of the Reds whooped and clapped. "Grace, that was amazing!"

"But we didn't win," Grace said quietly.

"Who cares?" Jenna blurted. "That was an incredible

shot." She smiled proudly at Nat, Tori and the rest of her teammates. "That was awesome teamwork out there. Keep it up."

"Great shot, Grace!" Alex said, walking over with Sarah.

Sarah nodded. "Good game, guys!" she said, and she and Alex shook hands with each of the Reds.

When Alex reached out for Jenna's hand, she hesitated for a split second, looking at Jenna's face uncertainly. Jenna closed the distance between them, shaking her hand. "That shot you made earlier was nothing but net, Alex. You played great."

"And *you* were a great coach for your team," Alex said. "I'm sorry you didn't get to play."

"Me too," Jenna admitted. She still felt a little frustrated that she hadn't gotten to play against Alex and give her and Sarah a run for their money, but she'd have more chances to do that. "There's always next year," she said with a smile. "And don't go getting too cocky over this win. The soccer tournament's tomorrow, and we're more than ready to take you on."

Alex grinned. "I can't wait."

Jenna led the way from the basketball court through the path of pine trees towards the bunks, and she got all the

Reds to start a cheer against the Blues as they walked. They were shouting and laughing so loud, they didn't hear the crackling of branches on the forest floor until it was too late.

"What was that?" Nat said, stopping mid-cheer.

"Probably just a deer." Jenna shrugged. "Don't worry ab—"

A blue water balloon shot out of the pine trees, headed straight for them.

"Duck!" Jenna yelled, too late, just as the balloon smacked into Tori's shoulder, exploding into a torrent of blue liquid.

Tori screamed, wiping at the blue liquid coursing down her face and arms. "It was filled with paint!" she cried.

"We're under attack!" Alyssa cried, just as a shower of blue balloons rained down on them from all directions. "Run!"

Jenna took off with everyone else, but she lagged behind because of her crutches and got pelted in the back twice. Luckily, her cast only got a little paint-splattered. She scoured the trees as she fled, but all she could see were flying balloons, not the sneaks who were launching them. When she broke out of the trees and into the clearing, she assessed the damage.

Almost every single one of the Reds had been hit.

"We look like a bunch of renegade Smurfs," she said, and everyone laughed as they wrung the paint from their clothes and hair. "I'll give you guys three guesses who on the Blue team masterminded this."

"We don't need three guesses," Grace said.

Alyssa, Nat and Tori all looked at each other and nodded. "Blake," they said together.

"You got it," Jenna said. "But there's no way we can prove it, not if the Blues won't talk."

And the Blues wouldn't talk. By the time the Reds had cleaned themselves up during the break between events and met the Blues on the camp lawn for the obstacle course group event, Dr. Steve had heard about what happened, but no one was naming names.

"Good sportsmanship is one of the things required of all of you during Colour War," Dr. Steve said, addressing everyone before the obstacle course competition started. "And the prank that the Blues pulled on the Reds earlier today was not in keeping with the rules of fair play. So, I'm deducting twenty-five points from the Blue team for unsportsmanlike conduct."

The Blues booed and hissed while the Reds cheered. The deduction erased the points the Blues had scored when they'd won the basketball competition, leaving the teams tied. Much to Jenna's frustration, though, the Blues still went on to win the obstacle course competition. But the Reds won the boating race. As the first day of Colour War came to a close, the Blues were ahead by just twenty-five points. Jenna crawled into bed that night knowing that tomorrow's soccer game and pie-eating contest were the two big chances the Reds still had to gain the lead. And all night long, she dreamed of eating pies filled with soccer balls, one after another after another.

CHAPTER TEN

Today was the day – the day that would decide the fate of the Red team for ever, and Jenna was ready. In just ten minutes the division soccer game would start, and she'd have to sit on the sidelines, waiting it out. Darn her broken leg! If only she didn't have this stupid cast, she'd be running onto the field with the rest of the Reds, getting ready to crush the Blues. But as she dabbed on a last dash of paint under her eyes, she knew that even if she wasn't playing, she certainly wouldn't be helpless, either. What she lacked on the field, she was going to make up for on the sidelines.

She stepped back from the bunk mirror, surveying what three containers of paint and about two hundred feathers had done to her appearance. She was transformed – a flash of flaming colour. She'd painted her face fiery red, she was wearing a red headdress left over from last year's drama production of *Peter Pan*, and her newly painted bright red cast was practically glowing under the fluorescent light. Today, she would be a Red warrior, fighting for her team. And no one would be able to stop her.

As she walked onto the soccer field, a hush fell over her teammates. Then, they all burst into cheers.

"I may not be on the field with you today," Jenna said, "but there was no way I wanted any of you to miss seeing me cheer you on."

"You'd have to be blind to miss that outfit," Chelsea said.

"So," Jenna said, "now's your chance to show the Blues what you can really do. That last play you made on the basketball court yesterday was awesome. If you play like that from the start today, you can win this game."

Grace shook her head doubtfully, her curls falling into her face. "Did you see Alex and Sarah warming up? If we get in the path of one of their balls, we're dead."

Nat nodded. "I'll never live to eat sushi again."

Anyone who knew Nat knew how serious that would be. She practically ate sushi for breakfast, lunch and dinner when she was back home in Manhattan.

"Simon said he might stop by to see me play after his division game is over," Nat said. "He's awesome at soccer. What if he thinks I'm awful when he sees me play?"

"And there's no way I can be a convincing Cinderella in the play tonight if a flying soccer ball breaks my nose," Grace said. She'd been practising her lines during all of her free time for the last week, and all the girls knew she'd be heartbroken if she didn't get her part just right.

"First of all, Nat, you're not awful, and you have lots of sushi to look forward to. And Simon will think you're even hotter when he sees you play! And Grace, you're going to be a gorgeous Cinderella, because the ball's not going to get anywhere near your nose." She grinned at her teammates. "Hey," she said to them, "soccer didn't kill me, did it?" She held up her leg.

With her red cast flashing on the sidelines like a beacon for all to see, Jenna yelled her lungs out as Natalie, Alyssa, Tori, Chelsea, Grace and the other girls took the field:

"We're gonna tear up these fields and win this fight,
Score lots of goals with Red team might.
The Blue team's going down as our score climbs higher,
We'll kick the Blue team's butt, 'cause we'll never tire!"

*   *   *

Natalie and Tori looked scared out of their minds as the game kicked off, but Jenna followed every move they made, pacing up and down the sidelines and shouting encouragement.

Within the first few minutes, Alex stole the ball from a fumbling Grace and raced to the goal with it for the first score of the day.

"That's okay!" Jenna said, urging Grace on. "Shake it off! Think of yourself as a ball magnet. Be one with the ball!"

Grace laughed, but soon enough, she was actually dribbling the ball with a little more certainty. She passed it seamlessly to Nat, who performed what looked like some sort of strange dance move to keep the ball away from Sarah, then dribbled the ball downfield and kicked a clean shot straight into the goal.

Whether it was Simon watching from the sidelines that had spurred Nat on, or just her growing courage, Jenna wasn't sure. But Nat was playing better than ever before. Near the end of the second half, the teams were tied. Alex and Sarah had each scored two goals for the Blues, but Perry, Tori and Chelsea had scored one each for the Reds, too.

"One more goal wins the game!" Jenna shouted hoarsely, starting to lose her voice from all the yelling. "You can do it!"

Alex and Sarah were bearing down hard on the ball, keeping it tight and close between them as they dribbled and passed to each other, getting closer and closer to the goal. But at the last second, Tori swooped down on Sarah and scooped the ball out from under her and raced away with it. Just as the Blues were closing in on her, Tori swung her leg back and sent the ball rocketing towards the goal with a power Jenna had never seen her use before. Gaby, the Blue's goalie, dived for the ball, but it brushed past her fingertips and sailed into the goal just as screams exploded from Reds.

"YES!" Jenna screamed, completely forgetting her crutches and hopping onto the field with her good leg to meet her teammates. "You won!" she yelled. "Victory!"

"I can't believe we won," Grace said.

"I can't believe you won, either," a voice said behind them, and they all turned to see Alex. "I just wanted to say congratulations on an amazing game," she said. "You all played great."

"So did you," Jenna said, high-fiving Alex. "And now the Reds and Blues are tied again."

Alex nodded. "Until the pie-eating contest."

Jenna smiled. "Finally! A game I can compete in."

"And one that I *can't* compete in." Alex smiled back. "Now I get to sit on the sidelines and watch *you*."

"It's about time." Jenna laughed. If she could win the pie-eating contest, the Reds would be in the lead. Her team had won one for her, and now she'd do her best to win one for her team. It was all up to her and her sweet tooth.

Her sweet tooth was starving, and so was she. Her stomach gave a loud rumble as she sat down at the table set up on the outdoor stage for the pie-eating competition. Jenna hadn't eaten one bite of lunch, because the last thing she'd wanted was to be scarfing down pies on an already full stomach. She'd seen some of the other kids eating their lunches, but as they sat down at the long pie table, too, she wondered just how much more they could fit into their bellies. As hungry as she was, she thought that winning this competition would be a piece of cake. Or a piece of pie, actually.

That was, until Adam walked onto the stage and sat down next to her.

"Are you ready to stuff your face, sis?" Adam asked with a grin.

"*You're* competing in this?" Jenna cried.

Adam patted his stomach. "Yup. And man, am I hungry. I didn't have breakfast *or* lunch today."

Jenna's spirits sank. Oh no. This was not good.

Adam was on the Blue team, and Jenna knew from witnessing his dozens of disgusting refrigerator raids at home that he was a bottomless pit. He ate all sorts of gross food, too. His favourite sandwich was pickles, peanut butter and Spam, for crying out loud! This competition had just gotten a whole lot tougher.

Andie stepped onto the stage with a megaphone. "Ladies and gentlemen, it's time for the pie-eating competition! Bring out the mystery pies, please!"

Mia and a couple of the other CITs walked out of the mess hall carrying huge trays holding half a dozen pies each. They stood behind the competitors with the trays so that the pies could be switched out quickly as they were eaten. "You have ten minutes to eat as many pies as possible!" Andie explained. Campers shouted cheers and clapped as the buzzer sounded.

When the first pie was put down in front of her, Jenna took one look and almost threw in her fork right then and there. With crumbly dirt crust and a few pink worms peeking out, the pie looked totally gagworthy! Worm pie?! No one had said anything about having to eat nasty worms, and these looked especially slimy and dirty, like they'd just been pulled out of the mud. Jenna heard the other kids at the table gasp as they looked at their pies, too. But these weren't real worms...they couldn't be. All she had to do was close her eyes and

161

take that first bite, and everything would taste just fine. She hoped. But what if she couldn't do it? What if she let her team down? Nope, she decided, that wasn't even an option.

She took a deep breath and dived in. After the first bite, a wide grin broke across her face. The pie was delish! That wasn't dirt...it was Oreo crumbs. And those pink worms were watermelon-flavoured *gummy* worms! This was her kind of pie – tons of sugar, tons of chocolate and mmmm good.

She scarfed down the whole thing and moved on to her second, third, fourth and fifth. From the corner of her eye, she could see the kids around her dropping like flies. The ones who had eaten lunch beforehand were the first to give up and leave the table. Next, it was the younger kids who just couldn't eat as much. But soon, it was just she and her bro, side by side, stuffing their faces.

By the eighth pie, Jenna's stomach was starting to get uncomfortably full, and the gummy worms weren't tasting nearly as yummy as they had before, but she didn't slow down. She looked up once to see Alyssa and Nat and Tori jumping up and down and screaming her name, so she pushed on, reaching for another pie, and another.

It was on pie number ten that Jenna noticed Adam

turning a very interesting shade of lime green. He froze, mid-chew, and bolted for the restrooms, leaving Jenna alone at the table – the winner!

The Red team burst into wild cheers as Jenna finished her eleventh pie, patted her belly, and let out a long, loud burp.

"Jenna Bloom has put the Red team back in the lead, ladies and gentlemen," Andie announced. Then she turned to Jenna. "How does it feel to eat eleven pies?"

Jenna took the megaphone. "Great!" she shouted. "I could eat eleven more right now!"

That afternoon the girls participated in a Scrabble tournament, and then finally that night was the camp-wide singdown. It all came down to this.

Jenna had never sung so loud in her entire life. The singdown had been going on for the last half-hour, and both teams were performing their final songs for the judges. Grace and Alyssa had written a song set to the music of ABBA's "Dancing Queen" titled "The Great Red Team", and the entire Red Team was singing its heart out. There were four CITs judging each song on execution, originality and camp spirit, and Jenna was positive that this song would win the war. She threw back her head and belted out the last verse:

"You can run, you can hide,
But the Reds will track you down,
Ooooh, you're in bad shape,
There's no escape, from the great Red team."

They finished the song, and Jenna grinned.

"There's no way the Blues can beat that song," she said to her teammates. "It's a winner."

Then, the Blues began their song:

"Camp Lakeview, duh duh duh, Camp Lakeview,
The pasta that they cook you, they say you should admire,
But when we tried a spoonful, our taste buds caught on fire,
Oh, we love our good old Camp Lakeview,
Even the mosquitoes,
And lake leeches that suck your toes,
We love our good old Lakeview.

Camp Lakeview, duh duh duh, Camp Lakeview,
The bunks that you stay in, they say are safe and clean,
But spiders bigger than dogs make homes in the latrine,
Oh, we love our dear old Camp Lakeview,
The mildewy shower heads,
And the bugs that share our beds,
We love our good old Lakeview."

As the Blues sang, Jenna had to admit that each verse was funnier than the last. Even Dr. Steve was laughing at the lyrics, and a few of the younger kids on the Blue team couldn't even get the words out of their mouths, they were giggling so hard.

As the song ended, Dr. Steve announced, "All of you did a fantastic job the last two days. The judges for the singdown competition will turn in their results to me shortly, and I'll announce the victor at the banquet tonight." He smiled. "But first, we're all in for a treat. This year's drama production of *Into the Woods* is going to be wonderful. I'll see you at the show."

Everyone groaned in disappointment, not wanting to wait a whole two hours before knowing who won Colour War, but soon everyone started walking to the bunks to get cleaned up for the play and the banquet. Before Grace, Tori and Brynn left to change into their costumes for the play, the other girls gave them hugs for good luck.

"I won't say 'break a leg'," Jenna said. "Because I've already broken one for you. I hope it brings you lots of luck."

"Thanks," Brynn said, and she, Grace and Tori headed off towards the drama room.

As the other girls went back to the bunks, Jenna hurried to the mess hall instead, to put the finishing touches on the decorations for the banquet. She and the rest of the banquet planning committee worked for the next hour hanging the Colour War banners, setting up the decorations and helping cook the food. When they finished, Jenna took one final look at the mess hall before leaving for the bunk. Everything looked amazing! She was so glad she'd been on the committee, because now she felt like she'd really done all she could to make sure this banquet would be the best ever. She couldn't wait to see the looks on everyone's faces when they walked into the mess hall. Tonight was going to be fantastic.

CHAPTER ELEVEN

"Come on, you guys! Hurry up!" Jenna yelled from the mess-hall stairs. Her friends were taking *for ever*, and she couldn't wait for them to see the fully decorated banquet hall. The banquet was the best part of Colour War, and in her opinion, anyone with two good legs should be *running* as fast as they could to get there.

They'd just come from the drama club's production of *Into the Woods*, and it couldn't have been better. The props and costumes had been fantastic – papier-mâché trees, velvet cloaks and sparkling fairy-tale dresses, and twinkling white lights that were strung across the stage as stars.

"Someday we'll all be able to see you and Grace and Brynn on Broadway," Nat said to Tori. "I just know it."

As Nat and the other girls finally climbed the mess-hall stairs, Jenna cried, "It's a miracle! You're actually going to make it to the banquet before my ninetieth birthday!" She grinned. "And thank goodness, because I'm starving."

Chelsea gawked at her. "I can't believe you're hungry after pigging out on eleven pies. That's disgusting."

Jenna grinned and knocked on her cast. "It's my hollow leg. I just can't fill it fast enough." She put her hand on the door to the mess hall. "All right, ladies, get ready to step into the streets of Rome, float down the canals of Venice, feast on pasta and pizza, and—"

"Jenna." Andie laughed. "Just open the door."

"Okay, okay," she said and swung the door open to the oohs and aahs of all the girls as they looked inside. A gondola decorated with flowers, paint and streamers sat in one corner in front of a mural of a Venetian canal, and kids were already lining up to have their picture taken sitting in it. Street lamps that Tiernan and Sarah had salvaged from the props from *Peter Pan* lined the aisles between the tables, and Pete had even turned a boat tarp into an awning that he'd hung over the window into the kitchen to make it look like the front of a real Italian café. Candles and Italian flags decorated every table, and the Leaning Tower of Pizza was especially impressive. Its twelve pizzas were stacked carefully one on top of another with breadsticks and leaning perfectly to one side. Red and blue Colour War banners covered almost every centimetre of the walls that wasn't decorated with Italian scenery, and red and blue streamers and balloons hung from the rafters.

"Wow!" Perry cried. "This is incredible."

"I think it looks just like Italy," Karen said.

Chelsea smirked. "Only someone who's never been to Italy would think that."

"And you've been to Italy, Chelsea?" Alyssa asked, to which Chelsea muttered a barely audible "no" that made Karen smile shyly.

"It looks good, doesn't it?" Jenna asked, forgetting Chelsea's snotty comment as she admired the decorations.

"Good?" Nat repeated. "It looks amazing!"

Jenna beamed. To think that originally she hadn't been that into helping with the banquet! Now she was so glad she had. "I want to show you something," she said. "Come with me."

Her friends followed her to a long table at the back of the mess hall that was loaded with cookies and Italian pastries. Pete had even tried to make cannolis, although he'd overdone it on the cream and they were looking a little soggy. But it was what was sitting in the centre of the table that Jenna really wanted her friends to see. It was a huge white cake with a red cougar and a blue bear painted on top with icing.

"It's the two Colour War mascots!" Nat said. "How cool is that?"

"It was Jenna's idea," Andie said, ruffling Jenna's hair. "She wanted to do something really special for dessert this year."

"The inside of the cake's red and blue, too," Jenna said proudly. "I swirled food colouring into the cake mix. And there's extra-chocolaty filling in the middle." She smiled. "You can *never* have enough chocolate!"

"I think it's the best banquet dessert we've ever had," Pete said, coming out of the kitchen to admire it.

Mia nodded. "No matter who wins Colour War, everyone will love this cake."

"We already do," Tori said.

As Jenna watched her friends laughing and talking at their table, she knew she'd done the right thing when she'd decided not to go through with her plan for Operation Drowned Rat. She'd put too much work into tonight to risk messing it up. And with such great friends, who needed pranks, anyway?

Of course, even without pranks, things got rowdy in the mess hall as everyone waited for Dr. Steve to announce the Colour War winner. Simon, Adam, Devon and Blake pounded on their table and shouted,

"Food, waiter, waiter, waiter, food!" as Andie and Kenny, the designated kitchen help for the evening, brought out trays of chicken parmesan, garlic bread and Caesar salad and put them on the buffet table.

"It looks like Pete and his fellow chefs totally outdid themselves this year," Alyssa said as they got in line for the buffet.

"Don't worry," Jenna said. "There'll be mystery meat tomorrow at breakfast. I'm sure of it."

As the girls sat down with their food, Dr. Steve took the stage.

"This year's Colour War competition was one of the closest in years," he began. "In fact, there was only a twenty-five-point difference between the two teams, which just goes to show how much good sportsmanship and effort everyone put forth."

Everyone in the mess hall broke into cheers, and a storm of fists pummelled the tabletops as the two teams chanted, "Red! Red!" and "Blue! Blue!"

Dr. Steve held up his hands for silence, waiting for everyone to settle down. "The final scores were 125 points for the Reds, and 150 points for the Blues. The champions in this year's Colour War are...the Blues!"

Alex, Brynn, Karen and Sarah all broke into wild whoops and screams, hugging and stamping their feet. Jenna, Natalie, Alyssa and Tori all hissed and booed but still couldn't help smiling at the Blues' happy delirium.

As the noisy chaos finally died down, Dr. Steve continued, "Congratulations to both teams on a Colour War well played. You all did a wonderful job, but as you all know, each year we recognize the players, by division, who have made an outstanding contribution to their team." He started with the younger kids first and worked his way up to Jenna's division. He held up two shiny medals. "The Most Valuable Player for the Red Team is Devon, and the Most Valuable Player for the Blue Team is Alex."

More cheers and clapping boomed through the mess hall as Dr. Steve hung the medals around Alex's and Devon's necks.

As soon as Alex had returned to her seat, Jenna ran over to give her a hug. "Congratulations," she said. "You were the obvious choice for MVP. All the way."

"Thanks. But...you're not jealous?" Alex asked tentatively.

"Are you kidding?" Jenna laughed and slapped her playfully on the shoulder. "I've never seen anyone play basketball and soccer the way you did the last two days. You totally deserve this. Besides, I know I only ate pie."

Alex laughed. "Yeah, well, that was impressive, too. I've never seen anyone eat pie the way you did today."

"Speaking of which," Andie said, walking over to

Jenna and putting an arm around her, "We have a little something for you, too."

"Really?" Jenna asked.

Andie pounded on the table to get the whole room's attention. "Tonight we have a special award for Jenna Bloom, who now holds Camp Lakeview's record for the most worm pies ever eaten in one sitting!"

Kenny handed Jenna a five-kilo jar of gummy worms. "Maybe that broken leg really *is* hollow," he said, "because it sure gave you an appetite!"

As applause broke out, Jenna took a dramatic bow and gave a victory wave with one crutch.

"Thanks for believing in me, guys," she said to Andie and the girls from both bunks. "If it hadn't been for all of you, I'd still be moping around here in pity-party mode." She put her tub o' worms on her chair. "Now, who wants cake?" she asked.

"I do!" Alex said with a grin.

Jenna hesitated. "But what about the sugar? Won't it make you sick?"

"I'm just going to have a little bite, and I won't eat any icing," Alex said. "It's your cake! I have to at least try it."

Jenna grinned. "Okay. But just one bite, and you'll have to wait your turn." She elbowed Alex playfully.

"I know. I know." Alex smiled. "Colour War rules."

It was a camp tradition that the winning team always served dessert to the losing team.

Jenna cut into her beautiful cake while Sarah, Alex and Adam waited, ready to pass out pieces to the Reds. But just as she was about to hand the first piece of cake to Alex, there were popping sounds from overhead.

"What—" she started, looking up.

Suddenly, the ceiling sprinklers all over the mess hall turned on full force!

Water rained down on everyone and splattered on the floor, tables and all over the plates of food and the beautiful, perfect Colour War cake. Everyone was screaming, laughing and yelling all at once. Some kids were running for the doors, but the whole mess hall had turned into a virtual Slip 'n' Slide. Red and blue streamers oozed colour onto the mess-hall floor, and the banquet cake started to look like an icing massacre.

"Jenna, your cast!" Andie yelled. "Try to keep it dry until I get back!"

"With what?" Jenna asked, but Andie had already run off in the direction of the supply closet. Jenna scooted to a chair and plopped down in it, ignoring the chilly puddle of water already accumulating in its seat. She propped up her leg so it was under a table, protected from the water. The only problem was, the rest of her *wasn't* protected, and now she couldn't move without getting her cast wet. So she sat back, letting the water pelt down on her, and watched the chaos around her, completely and totally stunned. How had this happened? This was *her* prank idea. How could someone else have had the same idea for Operation Drowned Rat? This couldn't have been just an accident, right?

"My hair!" Nat cried, trying to cover her head with her arms. Simon tried to come to her rescue, skidding towards her through the water, but Nat took one step towards him and slip-slided right into Tori. The two of them fell down in a soggy heap, until Simon was able to make his way over to help them up.

Some of the younger kids were laughing and stomping around on the slick linoleum floor, trying to splash each other. Sarah was skating around the floor on her sandals, trying to help some kids to the door. But already more than a couple of the third-year campers had fallen, and one of them had scraped his knees and was in tears.

Jenna was about to go help him, wet cast or not, when Andie slid over to her holding out an umbrella. "Come on," Andie said, holding the open umbrella over Jenna's leg. "Let's get you out of here."

They followed right behind Mia, who was ushering the rest of the drenched kids out into the warm night air.

"How did this happen?" Mia asked, staring bewilderedly into the soggy mess hall.

"Could something have set off the sprinklers accidentally?" Alex wondered.

Not something, Jenna suddenly realized, *someone*! Because just then she saw Blake rounding the corner of the mess hall, and he was as dry as a bone – and laughing! In a split second Jenna had the whole thing figured out. She'd thrown her notes for Operation Drowned Rat in the outdoor garbage that day...right outside her ceramics class. Blake must have found the plans in the trash and used them to carry out *her* prank!

Jenna couldn't believe it. She'd thought she and Blake were finally starting to be friends, but now he'd gone and ruined everything! The banquet she'd worked so hard on had turned into a demented water-park nightmare. The food, the decorations, everyone's clothes – completely ruined!

Suddenly, Dr. Steve exploded out of the mess-hall doors, dripping from head to toe, and shooting fire from his eyes.

"Jenna Bloom!" he said, his eyes flashing. "Are you responsible for this?"

"No, sir," Jenna started quietly. "It wasn't me, I swear." And this time, she was telling the absolute, total truth.

"Then how do you explain this?" Dr. Steve said, holding up Jenna's blurred and crumpled notes for Operation Drowned Rat. "I found them lying on the floor in the kitchen. Farrah told me this looked like your handwriting. Is that true?"

Jenna looked from one pair of angry eyes to another and sighed. So this was how it was going to come down. She might as well kiss any future years at Camp Lakeview goodbye, because there was no way Dr. Steve would ever believe she was innocent now. How could she ever explain this to him?

"Yes, sir," Jenna said. "It's my handwriting. But I threw that piece of paper away two days ago. I swear. I decided not to go through with the prank. Someone else must have done it."

She glanced at Blake, who now stood sheepishly a few metres away.

"If it wasn't you, then who was it?" Dr. Steve asked. "You're the only one here who could pull off something like this, and we have the proof right here."

Jenna just shook her head. It was hopeless. Dr. Steve would never believe his perfect little nephew Blake was actually the mastermind behind the mess-hall monsoon.

"Uncle Steve," Blake started, stepping forward and taking a deep breath. "It wasn't Jenna. I know it wasn't. Because it was—"

"Me," a voice said from behind them, and they all turned to see Pete, holding a spatula, his apron dripping a puddle onto the porch. "This was all my fault. I had a last batch of garlic bread in the broiler, and I forgot to set the timer. I got so into listening to the Colour War awards, I forgot all about it. By the time I remembered, the garlic bread was molten and smoke was pouring out of the ovens. I opened the kitchen windows, but it was too late. The second the smoke reached the sprinkler nozzles, it was all over."

"But, Pete," Blake started again.

"Don't protect me, Blake," Pete said sombrely. "I can take it like a man." He winked at Blake and Jenna.

Dr. Steve looked from Jenna to Blake to Pete. Finally, he let out a long, tired sigh. "All right," he said. "Jenna, I'm going to believe that your conscience overruled your prankster side and that you did actually throw these plans away. How they ended up in the mess-hall kitchen is a great mystery." He met Blake's eyes for one long moment, then rubbed his forehead and sighed again. "But...a mystery it will remain. Accidents do happen, and there's no use crying over spilled bug juice. We'll get this all cleaned up. I'm afraid I'm at a loss as to how to save our banquet, though. And the cake is a complete disaster."

Jenna stared out at the campgrounds, her mind

churning with ideas. "I've got it!" she cried. "It'll be perfect."

"Perfect is good," Dr. Steve said, brightening just a little. "I like perfect. Please share."

"Well, it's hot out here tonight," she started, "so maybe we can finally put this heatwave to good use. What about a bonfire down at the lake front?"

Dr. Steve rubbed his chin thoughtfully. "Not a bad idea."

"We can all get changed and meet down there in fifteen minutes," Jenna continued enthusiastically. "And I have the perfect solution for the cake, too. Just leave it to me."

She filled Dr. Steve in on the rest of her plan, and he and the counsellors rounded up the bedraggled campers, sending everyone off to their bunks to get out of their wet clothes.

Once Dr. Steve left to clean himself up, trailing droplets of water behind him as he walked away, Jenna turned back to Pete. "You didn't really burn any garlic bread, did you?" she asked him.

Pete smiled, shaking his head slowly. "Nope. But I figured every prankster deserves a second chance. You got one last year after you let the animals loose during the square dance, and Blake gets one now." Pete lowered his eyebrows at Blake in warning. "I saw you sneak out of the mess hall during the Colour War awards and pull those plans out of your pocket. I know it was you. But I don't imagine your uncle would be too happy with you if he found out the truth."

"No, he wouldn't," Blake admitted, and for the first time, Jenna got an inkling of how highly Blake actually thought of his uncle. He looked genuinely upset by the idea of Dr. Steve being unhappy or disappointed with him.

"Just don't pull something like that again," Pete said. "Got it?"

Blake blushed but nodded. Then he turned to Jenna. "You knew I set off the sprinklers, too, didn't you? Why didn't you turn me in?"

"Believe me, I thought about it," she scolded. But then she shrugged. "As a fellow prankster, I can appreciate a good prank when I see one. And that one ..." she grinned, "was the best prank ever. It's only fair that you get to stick around to see it go down in Lakeview history."

What came out of Blake's mouth next must not have been easy for him to say, because he sputtered and stared at the ground for a full minute before finally saying a simple, "Thanks, but I am sorry I ruined the banquet, even if it was a great prank. Your decorations were pretty cool."

"Was that a compliment?" Jenna asked, gaping.

"Sort of, but don't let it go to your head." Blake grinned.

"You know, I might be wrong," Jenna said, "but I think you're actually starting to like it here."

Blake shrugged. "Maybe I am."

"Truce?" Jenna finally said.

"Truce," answered Blake, shaking hands with her.

"Good," Jenna said. "Now, let's go save the final banquet."

CHAPTER TWELVE

Jenna dumped the final box of her candy onto the growing pile on the picnic table. A bonfire was roaring on the beach, throwing yellow sparkling light onto the lake. The counsellors had lined the waterfront with tiki torches, and everyone was sitting at the picnic tables, on the pier, and on towels in the sand, talking, laughing and having a great time.

"That's the last of it," she said, standing back to gaze in satisfaction at the mound of candy and platters of Twinkies, brownies, cookies and Rice Krispies treats covering every centimetre of the table.

"There's enough here to feed an army," Blake said after tossing his pillowcase full of Nerds and Twizzlers onto the pile.

"Do you think this will make up for the cake?" Jenna asked. For the past half an hour, Jenna and Blake had been recruiting other campers to donate the goody stashes from their bunks to make desserts for everyone for the final banquet. From the looks of the enormous pile, it seemed like just about everyone had pitched in a little something. Blake had helped Jenna carry both of her own boxes down to the lake front, too. Even Alex had goodies in the pile that she could eat – the special honey cookies that Jenna's mom had sent for her earlier last week.

"It more than makes up for the cake." Blake grinned. "We'll be on sugar highs for a week, at least."

"A broken leg does have some perks," Jenna said as she and Blake sat down with Natalie, Simon, Alyssa, Alex, Adam, Brynn and the rest of the gang to enjoy the junk-food feast. "My mom and dad felt so bad for me, they sent me twice as much candy as usual, just to get me through Colour War. There's even enough for everyone to have seconds!"

"Not if you start eating it," Chelsea grumbled, still angry about her favourite skirt getting drenched earlier, even though Andie had assured her that it would be fine. "You could probably finish off that entire pile."

"Nuh-uh," Jenna said. "Not tonight. Italian food is one thing, but I'm going easy on candy for a while. Those watermelon gummy worms put a temporary damper on my sweet tooth."

"Thanks to me," Blake snickered.

"What?" Jenna asked.

Blake's eyes twinkled. "The worm pies were my invention. I overheard Andie and Alex talking to Uncle Steve about it, so I came up with the kind of pie." He smiled. "You're not the only one who has brilliant ideas, you know."

"Oh, I know. That's what scares me." Jenna laughed. "I guess I should just be glad they weren't real worms."

Everyone laughed, except Nat, who was horrified by the idea.

"I can't believe camp's almost over again," Alex said. "For a whole year. That's for ever."

Adam smiled at her and reached over to give her hand a split-second squeeze. "It'll go by fast. You'll see."

Jenna couldn't believe what she was seeing! Her brother had practically almost held hands with Alex! Ick! But as Jenna watched Alex blushing in the firelight, she suddenly found herself smiling instead of gagging. Seeing Alex and Adam crushing on each other might take a little getting used to, but it was actually...sort of...cute? Of course, that didn't mean she was going to crush on any guy any time soon. No way. But at least now she'd be able to hang out with Alex and Adam without being totally weirded out.

"So, Jenna," Perry asked her. "What's the first thing you're going to do when you get your cast off?"

Jenna smiled. "Completely cream Alex in soccer."

"In your dreams," Alex said. "You couldn't do that even *before* you broke your leg."

"Wanna bet?" Jenna said. "What about last year when I kicked that ball right over your head straight into the goal, and the year before that, when I scored fifteen goals in the second half. And then there was the time when I—"

Alex burst out laughing. "I give up," she said, throwing up her hands. "I just wanted to see if your broken leg had affected your memory."

"Very funny," Jenna said drily, but she was smiling. "My soccer game might have to wait a few more weeks, but let's not forget who's the pie-eating queen." She ribbed Adam. "By the way, are you feeling better, bro? 'Cause I brought you something special to eat tonight." She popped open the five-kilo tub of gummy worms she'd won earlier and held it under his nose. "Mmmm, doesn't that smell good?"

Adam leaped up from the table, turning a shade paler. "Jenna, come on!" he said, holding one hand over his mouth and one over his stomach. "That's not funny!"

"If it's not funny, why is everyone laughing so hard?" Jenna said with a giggle as everyone cracked up.

"Ah," Andie said, grinning at the two of them.

"I sure am going to miss you guys and your sibling rivalry."

Jenna giggled again and looked around her. The stars were shining, fireflies were blinking, and the moonlight sparkled on the lake. A couple of the smaller kids fell asleep on their towels, and some of the counsellors had to carry them back to their bunks. But Jenna and her friends just huddled in closer to the bonfire as the night got colder, talking about all the fun they'd had over the summer, sharing pictures and home addresses, roasting s'mores, and telling ghost stories.

As Jenna ate her s'more, she looked around at all of her friends. There was Alex, her toughest competitor and veteran camp buddy; Nat, her favourite Manhattan fashion consultant; Alyssa, her reality check; Adam, her annoying but lovable (on occasion) twin; and Blake, her arch nemesis and...friend? After all they'd been through the last couple of weeks, was it possible that the guy she'd found so annoying and stuck-up at first had turned into someone she might actually have fun with? Maybe it was.

She handed him the second s'more she'd just made. "Thanks, Blake."

He blinked in surprise as he bit into the s'more. "For what?"

"For proving that I was wrong about you," Jenna

said, "by giving Lakeview a chance. And for pulling off Operation Drowned Rat."

Blake gaped at her. "What? But I thought you were mad at me for that."

Jenna shrugged. "I was, but not any more. Because if it hadn't been for you, none of us would be out here right now," she waved towards the bonfire, "enjoying all this. Don't get too cocky or anything, but you made this the best banquet ever."

"Until next year," Blake said with a mischievous grin. "Just wait until you hear what I've got planned. I'll need a partner in crime, though."

"I'm retired, remember? You'll have to find another accomplice." But then she leaned towards him. "But I can't wait to see what happens," she whispered with a grin.

After the bonfire, all the girls from both bunks crowded into 4A for a final night of girl bonding. Andie, Mia, Becky and Sophie had all agreed that the girls could hang out together for an extra hour before lights-out, and the bunk had turned into one huge slumber fest. Alex, Sarah, Brynn and all the other 4C-ers were sitting on the floor to make room for everyone. The bunk was completely packed and noisy, just the way Jenna liked it.

"So, are we going to have a camp reunion before next summer?" Jenna asked.

"Of course," Alyssa said. "Don't we always?"

"We could plan to get together for more than just the reunion, too. You could come visit me in Manhattan again," Nat offered. Last fall, all the girls had stayed in Nat's New York apartment for the whole weekend of the camp reunion, and it had been a blast.

"Maybe you want to try someplace different this year?" Andie asked.

"I know!" Tori said. "You could come to LA to visit me! I could take you to my favourite juice bar. They have the best banana-strawberry smoothies you'll ever have in your life."

"I don't know if smoothies can top New York pizza," Nat said. "That's the best food there is in my book, besides sushi, of course."

"And you're not biased or anything." Tori giggled. "You guys will love LA. We can shop till we drop and go to museums."

"I've heard that the theatre there is awesome, too," Grace said.

"I'll go," Jenna said. "On two conditions."

"What are they?" Mia asked.

"That I get this darn cast off first!" she said as everyone broke into laughter. "And...that there's only limited boy talk during our girl bonding time."

"But what if I kiss Simon for real and want to tell you guys?" Nat asked forlornly.

"You're limited to five minutes of details about boys... tops," Jenna said. *"Especially* if you kiss Simon for real."

"Fine by me," Alex jumped in.

"But won't you want to fill us in on what's happened with you and Adam?" Sarah asked Alex.

"Hey, I can do that in less than five minutes, no problem," Alex said. "Besides, I might like Adam, but my friends still come first."

Jenna smiled, relieved to hear that even if her friends were starting to get interested in boys, they would still be able to have just as much fun without them, too. "No matter where we meet up this year," she said, "we're going to have a great time, as long as we're all together."

"And we can use our camp blog until then, and we can e-mail each other, too," Brynn said. "We'll keep in touch, no matter what."

All the girls nodded as Mia handed out lists with everyone's home and e-mail addresses on them.

"Okay," Andie said, holding up the new fall preview issue of *Cosmo Girl*, "anyone want me to read the special ten-page autumn horoscope, 'Who will you fall for in the fall?'"

"I already know who Tori's falling for," Natalie said. She grinned slyly. "Blaaaake."

"I am not," Tori said, elbowing Nat. "I'll never forgive him for the toothpaste incident. No way."

"But Blake got his payback for the toothpaste," Jenna said, "and for the bucket of lake water in my shower, too." She held up the final issue of the camp newspaper for everyone to see. "Behold, Miss Camp Lakeview." She unfolded the front page to the photo collage of the summer, and there was Adam's photo of Blake, front and centre. In it, Blake was snoozing peacefully, his pomegranate lipgloss shimmering in perfect cover-girl form. "If anyone else needs a makeover, I work wonders."

"I'll pretend I didn't just hear that confession," Andie said, but she was smiling.

"He's a regular sleeping beauty," Alyssa remarked, and all the girls cracked up.

"He's even good-looking wearing lipgloss," Tori said, causing ten pillows to be launched at her head. "What? Maybe I *can* forgive the toothpaste incident. Just look at him! Who wouldn't crush on a guy like that?"

"I wouldn't," Jenna said. "He might be an okay prankster, but he's still a guy. Gross."

She pulled back the cover on her bed, slid between

the sheets, and suddenly felt dozens of pine needles pricking into her. "Ack! They're all over my mattress!" she cried, struggling to brush the itchy needles from her pyjamas.

"I bet I know who did that," Alyssa said. "Blake!"

"Jenna Bloom," Andie said. "I think you might have finally met your match."

"Not if I can help it," Jenna said, giggling. Right at that moment, a yell echoed from the direction of the boys' bunks.

Andie narrowed her eyes at Jenna. "What was that noise?"

"Don't worry," Jenna said innocently. "I think Blake's bed might have just mysteriously fallen apart. That's all. It's nothing that a few nuts and bolts can't fix."

"And where would those nuts and bolts be?" Mia asked.

"Under my mattress." Jenna smiled. "Hey, even a retired prankster gets to have one last laugh, right?"

Andie sighed, then giggled. "Just make sure it's really your last, okay?"

"I promise," Jenna said. "At least until next summer!"

Turn the page for a sneak
preview of more

SUMMER CAMP
SECRETS

FALLING IN LIKE

PROLOGUE

Posted by: Val
Subject: Candy War! & TRAUMARAMA!

Happy November, ladies of the Camp Lakeview
4A/4C Bunk Alliance! As your official blog
"Scream Queen", I'm checkin' in to say I hope
you all had a fab Halloween. I'm so glad we are
still staying in touch. Thank you to our
counsellors, Becky and Andie, for setting up this
two-bunk blog for us!

Okay, here are the results of our trick-or-treat
contest:

A big sugar high-five for Jenna! She won with
178 pieces, and that's not counting the sixteen
booger-flavoured Bertie Botts that her twin bro
Adam snuck into her sack. Chelsea was a close

second with 152. Grlz, you totally put the "puke" in Camp Lakepuke!

Now for Best Costume:

The winner is...Brynn, the White Witch of Narnia. She got "lucky thirteen" e-votes. As you can see from her pic, she looks...chilly!

So, do you guys want to do anything "together" for Thanksgiving?

On to my TRAUMA: Last Friday my Aunt Juanita had back surgery, so my mom flew to Maryland to take care of her for a few weeks. This means I have to stay full time with my dad, my stepmom Sharin, and my stepsister LaToya. As if that weren't bad enough...our brand-new low-flow toilet overflowed...and guess whose room it flowed into!

SO...I'm bunkin' with LT until my room is fixed. She has gone completely kookoo over my "invasion" of her "personal space". She says it isn't "fair" and I agree. I think it would be more fair if every shoe she owned got soaked with pee water! (J/K)

I hope you ALL will write lots of posts and e-mail/IM me so I can "retain a pleasant attitude" (my mom's words) until my mom comes home. I am trying really hard to roll with this but I'm pretty sure I'll need some support from my CLFs (Camp Lakeview Friends).

So, what's up with everyone else? I know you're all busy but we want to know what you're busy with!

KIT,

Val

CHAPTER ONE

Alyssa sat at a computer in her middle school's media centre and read Val's blog post. Poor Val was having a pretty tough time with her stepsister. Val didn't even like hanging around LaToya at her dad's house on weekends. Now she was stuck there 24/7 until her mom came home.

Alyssa wanted to write Valerie back right away to show her support, but the study hall bell was due to ring and she didn't want to be late for her art class. Today they were going to sketch an actual artist's model, and Alyssa could hardly wait!

I'll write Val tonight from home, Alyssa decided. With a glance at the clock above the mega-colourful mural of pioneer life, she powered the PC down. Then three...two...one! The bell trilled, signalling the end of the period.

Grabbing up her backpack and her charcoal-coloured puffy down jacket, Alyssa left the media centre. Her beaded chandelier earrings tickled her jaw line as she joined the chattering throngs of students in the main hall. She had "artist" written all over her look – along with the paint-flecked black T, she also wore a black jeans skirt, black boots and a cool black knitted cap she had found in her mother's old packed-away clothes. Her fingers sported cranberry-red polish, and her matching lipgloss was a total score from her favourite ninety-nine cent store.

Other kids rushing to their next-period classes surrounded Alyssa. Up ahead, Beckah and Rose, her art class BFFs, zoomed into the art room. Alyssa dodged around a group of boys and dashed in after them.

As she crossed the threshold, she skidded to a halt.

Wow.

A statuesque young woman was perched on a stool next to Mr. Prescott's wreckage of a desk. She was dressed in monochromatic indigo – a navy blue boatneck sweater and a pair of dark blue jeans – and her profile was very distinct – high forehead, ski-slope nose, a little overbite and a pronounced jawline. Her neck was as long as a giraffe's, practically. Alyssa assumed she was their model. All in all she was an art student's dream model, dramatic and exotic-looking.

Sweet!

Alyssa entered her sanctuary. The art room was her favourite place in the entire world. The walls were covered with student artwork, intermingled with prints by some of the greats – Degas, Cezanne, O'Keeffe, and the *Tar Beach* illustrations of Faith Ringgold. She inhaled the scent of creativity – a mixture of oil crayons, chalk, oil paints and clay dust. She said her hellos to Beckah and Rose as she took her chair across from them. The three buds were clustered in the middle of a big, long table they shared with seven other students.

There were a total of twenty-five students in the class. Everyone was pulling out their sketchpads and making a big deal out of selecting which pencil to use, even though they were all standard-issue No. 2s. Some of the boys were snickering as they glanced at the model, and Alyssa just rolled her eyes. Middle-school boys were *so* immature.

"This is going to be cool!" she said to the girls, pulling a ginormous rubber eraser from her heavily-stickered purple plastic art box and setting it next to her pencil. Mr. Prescott, her art teacher, liked to say that there were no mistakes in art. Maybe not, but there certainly were do-overs.

Beckah nodded excitedly. "I can't imagine posing in front of a roomful of people. I'm going to feel weird staring at her," Rose whispered.

"She's a *model*," Alyssa argued. "She's used to it."

"I would hate it," Rose insisted.

"That's why you're *not* a model," Beckah said.

The bell rang, and Mr. Prescott bustled in from the hall, balancing a stack of long, flat boxes of oil pastels and a stack of papers against his chest. His goatee, heavy eyebrows and buzz cut floated above his tower like a caricature drawn on a balloon.

"Good morning, *mes artistes*," he said, as he plopped everything down on his very messy desk. Alyssa wondered if it was true that there was an entire three-year-old pizza on the bottom layer of sketches, canvases, memos, posable wooden figurines, unopened paint cans and art books. That was the rumour.

"This is Willa Ackel, our model for this morning." The model smiled at Mr. Prescott and then at the class. "We'll begin sketching in a moment, so Willa, you can hang out. But first, let me tell you artists about a contest you are all invited to enter."

Alyssa raised her brows as she smiled eagerly at Beckah and Rose. An art contest? Rock!

"Some of you have heard of *Works*, our school arts quarterly," Mr. Prescott continued. "The first issue for this academic year will be out in a couple of weeks."

Alyssa nodded. *Works* was a great journal. She had pored over the last year's issues. Some of the art was good enough to hang in galleries. And the poems and short stories were fantastic. She hadn't had the nerve to submit anything of her own. After all, she had been a brand new middle-schooler.

Mr. Prescott continued. "Last year, the editors kept getting submissions from the same few people over and over. So this year's staff decided to run a contest to encourage more people to contribute. The prize will be a showcase in the next issue. There will be five pages of art from the visual arts winner, and five pages of stories, essays, or poems from the language arts winner."

"Whoa," Beckah murmured. "That's seriously cool."

"There are a few rules," Mr. Prescott said, "and you can only submit one entry. The deadline is in two weeks. If you're interested, please pick up a flyer after class."

Interested? Who wouldn't be?

Across from Alyssa, Rose crossed her eyes and wrinkled her nose as if to say, *No way*. But Beckah mouthed at Alyssa, *I'm in!*

Alyssa whispered back, "Me, too!"

"All right, let's get to work," Mr. Prescott said, clapping his hands together. He smiled at Willa, who sat taller on her stool.

Alyssa settled in, raising her arm over the blank piece of paper. She glanced over at Willa, making mental notes about her proportions as she got ready to make the first, defining line.

But to her surprise – and that of everyone else in the class – Willa climbed on top of the stool, raised her hands high over her head, arched her back, and gazed up at the ceiling.

"Oh," Mr. Prescott said raising his bushy eyebrows. "Interesting choice."

I totally love it, Alyssa thought. It was a magical moment – Alyssa could actually see her finished sketch in her mind as she looked from the model to the blank page and back again. It was as if she were working *with* Willa, and together they would make every pencil mark on Alyssa's sketch paper.

I'm in the zone! Alyssa thought, and quickly went to work.

Priya and Jordan stood like prisoners in front of Ms. Romero's desk in the science lab. She had her grade book open, and there was bad news.

Priya and Jordan had C's in science. C's were not good enough for their two sets of parents. They *had* to raise their grades or they would be grounded for the rest of their natural lives.

"Here's what I suggest," Ms. Romero said. "The

Tri-County Regional Science Fair is six weeks away, and if you can put together projects good enough to enter into the fair, I'll give you twenty points of extra credit."

That would give me a B, Priya calculated, *and J a B-minus.*

"We're in," Priya said, speaking for both of them. Jordan nodded like a bobblehead.

"Totally in," Jordan agreed. He smiled at Priya. "We need a team name. We'll be the Titans of Science."

"How original," Priya said, laughing. Their school mascot was the Titan.

"Wait." Ms. Romero raised her red pencil in the air, signalling a flag on the play. "I know you two are best friends. Do you think you will distract each other if you team up together to work on this?"

Priya and Jordan shook their heads in unison. "No way!" Priya said. "We'll help each other. We live next door, so we can meet after school every day without worrying about transportation and things like that."

Jordan nodded. "We do tons of stuff together. We even planned our camp trip to Washington DC, together."

"On the other hand," Ms. Romero continued, cocking her head in that way she had when she was thinking through all the variables of an experiment, "maybe it would be better for each of you to team up with someone who is a little stronger in science."

Their faces fell. No Priya and Jordan? No Titans of Science?

"Please?" Jordan begged. "We'll do an awesome job."

"We totally will," Priya promised.

"All right," Ms. Romero said. "We'll give it a try. But I want to see your progress, all right? I want you to come up with your project idea and fill out a proposal packet by Friday. That gives you all week. I'll look at it over the weekend and let you know next Monday whether or not you can proceed."

She leaned forward as if to emphasize her next words. "You need my okay to enter the fair."

"We will amaze you," Jordan promised.

"Just do a good job," Ms. Romero said.

Yes! Priya grinned at Jordan. He grinned back. Now they were next-door neighbours, BFFs *and* fellow mad scientists.

"Here's the proposal packet." Ms. Romero pulled out a drawer and extracted a thick stack of stapled pages. "Remember, I need it Friday."

"Got it." Priya took the papers from her and unzipped her backpack. She carefully slipped the packet into a dark purple folder and rezipped her pack.

"Thank you so much, Ms. Romero," Priya said. "We won't let you down."

To find out what happens next read

FALLING IN LIKE

Out now!

Complete your collection of

SUMMER CAMP
SECRETS

Pack the perfect summer accessory
in your beach bag today!

MISS MANHATTAN

City chick Natalie is surprised to find that she actually
enjoys summer camp – until her big secret gets out…
ISBN 9780746084557

PRANKSTER QUEEN

Mischievous Jenna is famous for her wild stunts, but this
year she's totally out of control. What's bugging her?
ISBN 9780746084564

BEST FRIENDS?

Fun-loving Grace starts hanging out with Gaby from rival
bunk 3C, before she realizes what a bully Gaby can be.
ISBN 9780746084571

LITTLE MISS NOT-SO-PERFECT

Sporty, reliable Alex seems like the perfect camper. But
she's hiding a problem that she can't bear to admit.
ISBN 9780746084588

BLOGGING BUDDIES

The girls are back home and keeping in touch through their
camp blog. But one bunkmate needs some extra support.
ISBN 9780746084601

PARTY TIME!

Everyone's excited about the camp reunion in New York! But when it gets to party time, will the girls still get on?

ISBN 9780746084618

THREE'S A CROWD

New camper Tori is from LA and is just as super-hip as Natalie. Good thing Nat isn't the jealous type – or is she?

ISBN 9780746093382

WISH YOU WEREN'T HERE

Sarah stresses when classmate Abby turns up at camp – will she expose Sarah as a geek to all her fun-loving friends?

ISBN 9780746093399

JUST FRIENDS?

Priya's best friend is a boy but she's sure she could never have a crush on him – until he starts to like another girl...

ISBN 9780746093405

JUST MY LUCK

When practical jokes start happening during Colour War, Jenna is the obvious suspect. But could someone else be to blame?

ISBN 9780746093412

FALLING IN LIKE

Valerie's wicked stepsister, Tori's forbidden crush, Alyssa's censored artwork...life back home after camp is so complicated!

ISBN 9780746093429

ON THIN ICE

Tori's only allowed to invite five friends on her fab holiday weekend. But how can she choose without hurting anyone?

ISBN 9780746093436

All priced at £4.99

Fancy some more sizzling Summer Camp fun?

✻ Try out Natalie's favourite magazine quizzes and learn how to draw like Alyssa

✻ Discover Jenna's recipes for the best-ever s'mores and Sarah's hottest tips for the most fun things to do on holiday

✻ Get the lowdown on all the best bits of Camp Lakeview, from the girls' fave games to tried-and-true campfire songs

✻ Plus, look out for fab competitions, and even get the chance to star on the Summer Camp Secrets website yourself!

It's all at

www.summercampsecrets.co.uk

Check it out now!